Midlife Crisis

Midlife Crisis

La Jill Hunt

www.urbanbooks.net

Urban Books, LLC
300 Farmingdale Road, NY-Route 109
Farmingdale, NY 11735

ISBN 13: 978-1-60162-129-0
ISBN 10: 1-60162-129-9

First Trade Paperback Printing May 2019
Printed in the United States of America

10 9 8 7 6 5 4 3 2 1

Distributed by Kensington Publishing Corp.
Submit Orders to:
Customer Service
400 Hahn Road
Westminster, MD 21157-4627
Phone: 1-800-733-3000
Fax: 1-800-659-2436

Sylvia

"Hello?" Sylvia whispered into the phone. It was more like a question than a greeting because she was wondering if the phone was really ringing or whether she had been dreaming. No one ever called their home phone.

"May I speak with Garrett Blackwell?"

Sylvia leaned over and stared at the alarm clock on the nightstand. It was almost four in the morning.

"Excuse me? Who is this?"

"My name is Elizabeth, and I'm a nurse at Mercy Hospital. I'm calling to speak with Garrett Blackwell."

"He's not in. He's traveling on business. Mercy Hospital, where is that?" Sylvia asked. She had never heard of it, so she knew it couldn't be located in the area.

"We are in Drakeville," the woman said. "Is there a number where Mr. Blackwell can be reached?"

"Drakeville? What's going on?" Sylvia asked. She was now wide awake and started sitting up to turn on the lamp. Drakeville was over four hours away from their home.

"There's been an accident, and Mr. Blackwell is listed as the next of kin for Miranda Meechan."

"Who?"

"Miranda Meechan," the woman repeated.

"I'm sorry. I don't know anyone by that name," Sylvia told her.

"Is there another number where Mr. Blackwell may be reached?"

"I will reach him and give him your information." Sylvia reached into the nightstand and fumbled for a piece of paper. She wrote down the name and number of the hospital then quickly dialed Garry's cell phone number. Her husband of nearly twenty years was a district manager for Xerox and often traveled for business.

"Baby, what's wrong?" Garry answered without even saying hello. She knew he had to be just as frightened by this early morning phone call as she was.

"Garry, Mercy Hospital just called asking for you."

"What? Why?" he asked.

Sylvia imagined her husband frowning and squinting because he didn't have on his glasses and was blind as a bat.

"They said you're the next of kin for someone named Miranda Meechan. I don't know who that is. Do you?"

"Who?"

"Miranda Meechan."

"Miranda Meechan," Garry repeated, and then said, "Baby, I don't know who that is or what they could be calling me for. I don't know."

"Me either, Garry. I told them they probably had the wrong number."

"How did they get your number?" he asked. "That's weird."

"They called the house." Sylvia nestled back under the covers. "I have the number if you wanna call them back."

"Naw, no need. You already told them they had the wrong number. Where is Peyton?"

"Garry, it's almost four in the morning. Where do you think she is?" Sylvia answered.

"I guess that was a dumb question, huh? She's doing exactly what you and I both need to be doing. Sleeping."

"Well, I hope that's what she's doing. You know I looked on Facebook one night last week, and she liked somebody's pictures at three in the morning. That child, I swear—" Sylvia sighed.

"What? You didn't tell me that when I was home this weekend. Whose pictures? It better not have been some knucklehead. I keep telling you that we're gonna have to monitor her with this internet stuff, Sylvia."

"Calm down, Garry. I didn't tell you because it was already handled. She's a seventeen-year-old honors student and athlete, and she's never been in any type of trouble. She's headed to college and has a successful life ahead of her."

"I know that, Sylvia. That's because we raised her right, but that doesn't mean we can slack off. If anything, we need to keep a closer eye on her."

"Good night, Garry," Sylvia told her husband.

"Good night, Syl. And Syl, you are doing an amazing job raising our daughter. You know how much I love and appreciate you, right?"

Sylvia smiled. She knew that Garry loved her and Peyton. Over the years, she learned to pick her battles. It was easier to just let Garry talk and move on.

"I love you too, Garry."

"Still?" he asked, as he had done every time since the first time she told him nearly twenty years ago.

"Still," she said, and they hung up.

"Mom, can you pick me up late tomorrow?" Peyton asked the next morning as they headed out the door. Sylvia had a full day ahead, and dropping her daughter off at school, as she had for the past twelve years, was the first thing on her agenda. Even though the school bus picked kids up right on the corner, Sylvia enjoyed the time they shared during the drive. It was their bonding time. She used the time to talk about current events and celebrity gossip that they heard on the morning radio shows, and she tied it in with real-life situations and scenarios. At times, Sylvia used the subjects as teaching moments, pointing out acceptable and unacceptable behavior.

"Why?" Sylvia asked, checking her phone again to make sure her ringer was on. She had tried to reach Garry, but he didn't answer. Normally he called both of them before they left the house, but this morning, he didn't.

He probably overslept. After all, I did call and wake him up at four this morning, she thought. But deep down, something didn't feel right.

"We're having a meeting about our community service for our senior projects."

Peyton's school required all graduating seniors to complete a minimum of sixty hours of community service and do a presentation based on their experience. When she first heard about it, Sylvia thought the hours were a bit excessive. After learning more about the requirements and seeing the projects that previous students had completed, she agreed that it was a great idea. She had spoken with one of the women at their church about having Peyton volunteer with the senior citizens group over the next few weeks.

"Fine," Sylvia agreed. She made a mental note not to forget and was grateful that it allowed her a few more hours to complete the tasks she had already scheduled, most of which involved her upcoming vow renewal. She thought planning her twentieth-anniversary wedding ceremony would be easier than planning her first wedding, but she quickly found out it was just as exhausting.

"Thanks," Peyton said, turning up the radio and listening to the local radio station's topic of the day, which was infidelity. The caller was a woman who said that she always told her husband if he ever cheated, it would be better if he was up front and honest about it, rather than have her find out some other way and he lie about it.

"Why would you want your husband to tell you he cheated? That's crazy." Peyton shook her head. "Who does that? You're gonna betray my trust and then brag to me about it? I don't think so. She's stupid. She basically gave him permission to cheat."

Sylvia laughed. "I don't think you understand. It's not about him cheating. No one wants their spouse or significant other to cheat. Her point is if he did make the mistake of cheating, be a man about it and tell her. Don't lie and say it didn't happen or let someone else be the bearer of bad news. She wants him to own his behavior."

"Nope. I'm not buying it. If my boyfriend cheats on me, he better know better than to come and fess up, because once I find out, I'm going for the jugular, and I'm trying to kill him!"

"What boyfriend? Is there something going on I should know about, young lady? Last I heard, there was no boyfriend. Only friends. Is it that guy whose pics you liked the other night at midnight? What's his name again so I can send him a friend request?"

"Oh my goodness, Mom. No, there's no boyfriend. And I'm not telling you his name. I can't believe you are all on my page like that anyway. You're almost as bad as Daddy."

Sylvia looked over at Peyton. "Oh, really?"

"Okay, you're definitely not that bad. He's way worse." Peyton laughed. They pulled up to the school, and she leaned over and gave her mother a kiss. "See ya, love ya, bye!"

"See ya, love ya, bye," Sylvia repeated. She pulled off and turned the radio back up, which was now playing

Keith Sweat. Her phone rang, and she answered thinking it was her husband.

"Oh my God. Is it true? Please tell me this is not happening to you."

"What are you talking about?" Sylvia asked her best friend, Lynne.

"I just talked to my mother. She said that you told Auntie Connie she can come and stay a few weeks."

"Yes, it's true. Good news travels fast, huh?"

"You must be a glutton for punishment. I can't believe Garry agreed to her coming in for that long. You know it'll be at least three or four months until her place is ready, right?"

"I know, but it may be sooner than that. And I haven't mentioned it to Garry yet. I am gonna wait and tell him when he comes home this weekend."

"Boy, I wish I could be a fly on the wall when you tell him that one. You know he don't like no one in his house, not even family. That man . . . I swear. He will give you the shirt off his back, but when it comes to that house, it's a whole 'nother story."

Sylvia thought about the phone call she had gotten in the middle of the night, and now, her husband's sudden unavailability. It didn't sit well with her.

"Hellllooooooo," Lynne sang out. "Are you here?"

"Yeah, let me call you back in a little while," Sylvia said and hung the phone up before Lynne could respond. She tried Garry's cell twice more. It no longer rang but went straight to voicemail. She didn't leave a message. She hit the screen of the radio, changing it to GPS, and routed her destination as Mercy Hospital. Keith Sweat was definitely right about one thing: *Something just ain't right.*

Sylvia

"Can I help you, dear?" the white-haired woman at the patient information desk asked. Her cheerfulness did nothing to calm the nerves Sylvia felt in her stomach. Suddenly, the master plan she'd created in her mind during the three hour and twenty–minute drive to the hospital was now gone. She tried to think.

"Good morning. It is still morning, isn't it?" Sylvia looked down at the gold Movado watch Garry had given her last Valentine's Day.

"Well, for the next fifteen minutes it certainly is," the woman said. "Are you here to see a patient, or do you have an appointment?"

"Um, a patient," Sylvia told her.

"Great. What's the patient's name?"

"Miranda, Miranda Meechan."

The woman typed on the computer keyboard, glanced up at Sylvia, and frowned. "She's in ICU. Well, she's actually in surgery right now. Are you family?"

"Yes, I am," Sylvia lied. When she heard ICU, she knew there was a risk of being told only family could be seen by the patient.

"Do you have an ID?"

Fumbling in her purse, she found her driver's license and passed it across the desk. The woman looked at her name, then the computer screen.

"Sylvia . . . Blackwell," she murmured and clicked the mouse. "There's a Garrett Blackwell in the ICU waiting room already."

Hearing that Garrett was already at the hospital took Sylvia by surprise. She sucked in her breath slightly and then nodded and said, "Yes, he's my . . . brother."

The woman scanned a copy of the card and then passed it back to Sylvia along with a sticker that read *Visitor* and an ICU room number. "Take the elevator to the ninth floor, and when you get off, go to the left. The surgical waiting area is right there."

"Thank you." Sylvia nodded then headed to the elevators.

She hated hospitals. She had spent enough of her early adulthood in and out of them. Her father was a hardworking man. He was a few years shy of retirement from the shipyard when he was diagnosed with asbestos poisoning. Sylvia was only twenty-three when he died. Her mother, who spent years washing her father's uniforms, died less than two years later of lung cancer. It was the most difficult time in her life, and most days she didn't know how she would make it. Garry was right there by her side, not only holding her hand, but holding her up when she could barely stand. He had been her rock.

She braced herself as she walked toward the entrance of the surgical waiting room, nearly bumping into an older, bearded gentleman dressed in green scrubs as he brushed past her.

"Oh, I'm sorry," she told him.

"No, it's my fault." He smiled and continued walking. He entered the same open glass door that she was headed to, and as she got closer, she caught a glimpse of Garry walking over and shaking the man's hand.

Sylvia inched closer until she was within earshot and listened, wondering if they could hear her heart, which was beating hard and loud.

"Mr. Blackwell, we did the best that we could, but it's still touch and go at this point. As you already know, there was a lot of internal bleeding and extensive damage to Ms. Meechan's chest and abdomen. Only time will tell at this point."

Sylvia saw the stress and strain in Garry's face as he listened to what the doctor was telling him. She could see that he hadn't slept all night.

"Right now she's in a coma. All we can do is wait," the doctor continued.

"I understand." Garry nodded.

"But your daughter is resting in the post-surgical recovery room, and she's going to be fine. You can see her in a couple of hours."

"Thank you," Garry whispered.

Your daughter . . . daughter . . . daughter. . . .

The words seemed to echo over and over as Sylvia stood watching the two men talk. She closed her eyes, praying that she was dreaming and not standing there catching her husband in the biggest, most confusing lie he had ever told.

Just as she was about to go and confront him about what was going on, a mass confusion broke out. There was an announcement of some code over the intercom, and Sylvia could hear beeps coming from down the hallway. She turned to see nurses pushing a large machine into one of the rooms. The doctor came running by, and right behind him, she saw her husband. His eyes met hers just as he was about to pass her, and then he stood frozen, as if he didn't know what to do. His eyes went from the direction of where the hospital staff was headed then back to Sylvia. She decided to make the decision easy for him and fled to the elevator.

"Sylvia! Sylvia!"

She heard him calling just as the doors closed and she pressed the button for the first floor. The millions of thoughts and questions in her head came faster and faster as the elevator stopped on each floor. People got on and off, chattering and smiling, causing Sylvia to want to scream, "Shut the hell up so I can *think*!" The doors had barely opened when they finally arrived on the first floor before she squeezed her way out and rushed toward the exit.

Where the hell did I park? she thought, trying to get herself together. She recalled taking a parking ticket out of the machine, but she couldn't remember what floor she'd parked on.

Think, Sylvia, think.

"Sylvia! Stop!"

She turned and saw Garry running toward her, and she took off toward the parking area. She blinked away tears as she tried to think of what numbers were on the cement pole she had parked in front of. She recalled parking beside a green Camry, or maybe it was a Taurus.

Think, Sylvia.

As she reached into her purse to retrieve the ticket, she felt someone pulling on her arm.

"Get the fuck off of me, Garry!" She snatched away.

"Please wait, Sylvia. I'm trying to talk to you!"

"Talk to me? Are you crazy? Have you lost your mind? There is nothing to talk about!" Sylvia snapped as she pulled her purse back on her shoulder.

"Don't be like that. I just need for you to listen to me," Garry said, reaching for her again.

"Don't put your damn hands on me, Garry. I mean it."

A security officer pulled up to the area where they were standing and asked if everything was okay. Sylvia nodded, and the guard gave Garry a questionable look.

"Man, my wife already told you everything was fine. Can we have some privacy, please?" Garry demanded.

"It's fine, sir," Sylvia told him. "I'm just looking for my ticket so I can get out of here." Her fingers finally touched the small, smooth item she was looking for, and she pulled it out and showed the guard.

"Yes, ma'am," the guard said after a few seconds and then left.

"Asshole," Garry said when he was a little farther from them. Then he turned to his wife and said, "Baby, please let me explain."

"There is no way you can explain this, Garry," Sylvia said to him in disbelief. "There can't be any reasonable explanation. Furthermore, I don't care to even stand here and listen."

Garry's cell phone began ringing, and he removed it from the leather case he wore on his belt. "It's the hospital."

"Oh, so your cell does work. I'm sorry. I wasn't aware of that, because I've been calling it since this morning, and you haven't answered the damn phone. But I see why. Go ahead and answer it! Better yet, get your ass back upstairs and take care of your family, you bastard!"

Three C, she suddenly remembered. *That is where my damn car is.* She didn't give Garry a second glance as she fled away.

Sylvia

When she finally arrived home, Sylvia sat on the side
of the bed for what seemed like hours. She didn't know
what to do, where to go, or how to even begin process-
ing what was happening. She reached into her purse and
pulled out her cell phone and stared at it.

*Who's the first person you're supposed to call when
you find out your husband has been cheating on you?*
She had been wondering that ever since she pulled out
of the hospital parking lot, and she still didn't have an
answer.

Her thoughts turned to her mother. It nearly scared her,
because she had been gone so long. Normally, when she
thought of her, it was when she came across something
that reminded her of the loving woman who had dedicated
her entire life to taking care of her family. Sylvia aspired to
be like her. She had been so strong, even in death, making
sure Sylvia knew exactly how everything had already been
arranged, from the funeral and her last will and testament
to the financial accounts she had set up for Sylvia and her
sister, Janelle. Her mother had been gone almost as long
as she and Garry had been married. Sylvia wished she was
still living; then again, this was so incredibly unbelievable
that maybe even her mother wouldn't have an answer for
her.

*What advice do you give your daughter who has
just found out her husband was cheating?* Her mother
probably would be just as shocked and confused, espe-

cially because Garry was so much like her father: strong, loving, and kind. Both men were damn near perfect, or so she had thought. Now, she wondered if her father had had any indiscretions of his own that she'd never known about. Janelle and Sylvia often said that their parents weren't just happily married, but blissfully married. Sylvia couldn't recall them even arguing one time. They were made for one another, just the same way Sylvia thought she and Garry were.

Now it seemed as if she didn't know the man that she was married to. The man she married couldn't possibly have been involved in an inappropriate conversation with another woman, let alone a child. There had to be some mistake. She had to have heard the conversation all wrong. But as she thought about the scene she had witnessed hours ago at the hospital, she knew that the word "daughter" had come out of the doctor's mouth, and Garry didn't object nor correct him.

Sylvia looked down at the phone again as it lay on the edge of the bed. There was no one she could call. No one to talk to. She was confused, dazed, alone, and most of all, she was heartbroken. She slowly stood up, closed the blinds, and closed the door of her bedroom. As she climbed into bed, she threw the phone across the room and heard it bounce against the wall. Pulling the covers over her head, Sylvia drifted into a deep sleep and prayed that she would wake up from what had to be a nightmare.

Tap, tap, tap.

"Mom, are you a'ight?"

Sylvia's eyes fluttered open at the sound of knocking on her bedroom door. "I'm fine, sweetie. What time is it?"

Peyton walked into the room dressed in a pair of leggings, an oversized T-shirt, and a pair of Ugg boots. "Almost ten. You've been 'sleep a long time."

"Wow. I didn't realize it was that late." Sylvia sat up. Her head was in a fog, and she thought that maybe the events from earlier that day had been a dream.

"Are you sure you're okay?" Peyton asked, then picked something up off the floor. "See, I told you, you sleep wild. You kicked the phone off the bed so hard that the battery popped out."

Seeing the phone made Sylvia remember throwing it and why. Tears began to form, and she hurried out of bed and ran into the bathroom, not wanting her daughter to see that she was upset. Peyton . . . her daughter . . . their daughter . . . their family. It was all too much. Sylvia sat on the commode and knew she had to talk to someone. She closed her eyes and began to pray.

God, please help me deal with this. I don't know what to do or who to turn to but you. Help me.

The house phone rang, and Peyton announced that it was Lynne, Sylvia's best friend, demanding to speak to her. "I told her you were in the bathroom, Ma, but you know how Aunt Lynne is," Peyton said, passing the phone through the bathroom door.

"Hey," Sylvia said. Her voice cracked, so she cleared her throat.

"Hey? Is that all you can say? Heffa, where the hell have you been? I've been calling your ass all day, and you stood me up! I don't have time to be going through all this. It ain't my damn wedding, vow renewal, whatever the hell it is we're planning! Now see, you're gonna mess around 'til the last minute and stuff not gonna be right, and watch you try to blame that on me. I finally got an appointment with the wedding planner my coworker used. You said you were gonna call me back, and I ain't heard from you!"

"I'm sorry," Sylvia told her. With all the chaos that had transpired, Sylvia had completely forgotten that they had a meeting with the florist. "Something came up."

"Sylvia Janese Blackwell, we have been talking about planning this twentieth anniversary shindig for over a year. Now it's time to get to planning, and you're acting weird. What could have possibly come up?"

Their anniversary. Twenty years. They had been planning it for over a year. Out of all their friends and family members, Sylvia and Garry were one of the few couples that had made it. Everyone else was divorced, remarried, or just straight-up single. They were survivors, and everyone wanted to be a part of the celebration. Now, Sylvia wasn't even sure who the hell the person was that she married. Here this man had another woman and a daughter that she had no clue about. Her heart became heavy, and there was no fighting the tears this time. Sylvia bawled into the phone.

"Sylvia, what's wrong? Oh my God, please don't tell me you're turning into one of those Bridezillas and having an emotional breakdown. We are too old for that, and I can't take it."

"No. Garry . . . he—I went to the . . . Mercy Hospital. . . ." Sylvia tried to talk, but she was crying too hard.

"What? Garry's in the hospital? What happened? Is he all right?"

"No, he's fine. He . . . there was an accident."

"Garry was in an accident?"

"No."

"Sylvia, stop crying. I don't know what you're saying. You know what? I'm on my way. Unlock the door and have some damn wine waiting for me when I get there."

Sylvia was grateful that Peyton had made herself dinner and was shut up in her room by the time Lynne arrived twenty minutes later. Her best friend had barely made it through the door when Sylvia began crying again.

"Sylvia, girl, please calm down and tell me what happened. Wait, let me get some wine first. Hell, you look like you need some yourself."

They grabbed a bottle of wine and two glasses and headed out into the enclosed sunroom. Sylvia looked out the window and into the clear water of the custom-designed in-ground pool as Lynne poured her a glass.

"Okay, talk."

Sylvia's eyes never left the water as she told Lynne everything without taking a breath. When she finished, she gulped the entire glass down in one swallow and said, "I don't know what to do."

"Whew, chile! Well, first of all, we needed liquor for this conversation, not pinot grigio, that's for damn sure. But that's neither here nor there. What you need to do is talk to your husband and find out who the hell this woman is and why the hell do they have a daughter. How old is this daughter?"

"I don't know." Sylvia shrugged. "And I don't care. I don't want to talk to him. He has a damn daughter by some other chick. What the hell do we need to talk about? My divorce settlement? How much alimony I'm gonna get?"

"If that's what you want, then yep. And he needs to explain all of this," Lynne told her.

"I don't want him to explain," Sylvia told her.

"Yes, you do. I get it—right now you're pissed, and rightfully so. I would say you are handling this quite well, because a sister like me woulda went slam off in that damn hospital right then and there on the spot. But you didn't. So, not only do you deserve an explanation, but you deserve an opportunity to go off on his ass. Hell, he ain't my husband, and I wanna go off on him. And you know I will be doing just that, by the way."

Sylvia realized that Lynne was right. She did deserve an explanation, even if she didn't want one. She deserved to know who this woman and her child were and where they came from. She deserved to know why he was listed as her next of kin. She deserved to know why he had lied when she asked him if he knew who she was after the hospital called in the middle of the night. Most of all, she deserved to know what other secrets he had been keeping from her.

Later the following morning, after Peyton had been dropped off at school and her routine morning errands had been completed. Sylvia sat at the desk of her home office, staring at her computer screen when she heard the front door open and the emotionless voice of their alarm system confirm that someone had entered. She heard the sound of keys being thrown into the bowl lying on the table in the foyer. Any other time, the familiar sounds of her husband coming home would excite her, but Sylvia didn't move. She just stared at the screen. Even when she felt his presence as he entered the room, she still didn't turn around.

"Sylvia."

Sylvia didn't respond. She could feel him coming closer.

"Sylvia."

"What!" she said with so much anger in her voice that she damn near scared herself.

Garry paused for a few seconds and finally said, "I need to know if you're ready to talk."

Again, Sylvia didn't say a word. She just slowly turned her chair around and stared at her husband. She could see the fatigue and exhaustion in his face. He was dressed in a Nike sweat suit and sneakers. He hadn't shaved, and the stubble was covering his chin and jawline. Sylvia almost felt sorry for him and almost reached out for him, but she glanced at the hospital visitor sticker on his shirt and was quickly reminded of why he was so tired.

"I love you. You know that I love you and Peyton more than life itself, and there is nothing I wouldn't do for you. I don't want you to doubt that for one second. I also know that the facts don't excuse the mistake that I've made."

"Mistake? Is that what you call this?" Sylvia snapped.

"Maybe *mistake* is the wrong choice of words. But essentially, that's what it is. It was a simple error in judgment that resulted in—"

"Garry, have you lost your damn mind? How the hell are you gonna stand there and try to rationalize this shit for me? Who are you trying to convince? It must be you, because that shit is *not* working for me. An error in judgment my ass!"

Garrett stared at her, not knowing what to say.

"Who the hell is she?"

"She's . . . she . . . her . . . we—" Her husband, who was never at loss for words, was unable to put two words together and form a complete sentence.

"Let me see if I can make it easier for you since that question seems to be too difficult for you to answer. Hmmm, let's start with something really simple. Tell me her name."

"You already know her name."

"Don't tell me what the hell I know! I asked *you* to tell me her name!"

Garry hesitated and finally said, "Her name is Miranda. Miranda Meechan."

"Miranda Meechan," Sylvia repeated. "And what's her daughter—I'm sorry, what's you and Miranda's daughter's name? Is it just the one daughter, or do you all have more children that I don't know about?"

"There's just one. Jordan."

Jordan. It was the name that she and Garrett had discussed and said they would choose for their next child, girl or boy, had there been another. But there hadn't been any more children—well, not for her.

"And how old is Jordan?" Sylvia asked, inhaling in an effort to prepare herself for his answer. She imagined a toddler, lying helplessly in a hospital bed while her mother fought for life and her father, who happened to be Sylvia's husband, stood there looking worn and desolate.

"Syl." Garrett reached for her, but she pulled away.

"Answer me!"

"She's fifteen." His voice was barely above a whisper.

"Did you say *fifteen*?"

"Yes." Garrett nodded.

The tears she had been fighting fell from her eyes. *Fifteen.* They had been married for nineteen years, and at least fifteen—no, sixteen of them—had been a lie. All of it was a lie. Garry and this woman Miranda—

Miranda! As if in a flash, Sylvia suddenly remembered that past New Year's Eve. They were hosting a get together at their home, and it had just turned midnight. After their traditional kiss, they were all sharing their well wishes when Sylvia saw her husband answer his phone.

"Happy New Year, Randy!"

She hadn't thought much of it, because it was one of many times she had overheard him talking to someone by that name. For years, he had spoken to or of Randy. It had never dawned on her that it was a woman. As she realized that this same Randy was her husband's mistress, Sylvia's world seemed to crumble even more.

Lies, all lies.

"Get out, Garry!" she screamed. "I want you out right now! Get your shit and get the fuck out of my house."

Sylvia heard Garrett's phone ringing as she ran out of her office and into their bedroom. She paced back and forth, rubbing her temples. This couldn't be happening. It had to be some horrific nightmare, and she would soon wake up. Had there been signs all along and she was too dumb not to notice? Had she been one of those stupid women so caught up in her own little world that she didn't realize her husband had been having an affair damn near as long as they had been married? All of this was too much to bear; too much for her to deal with.

"Sylvia, please."

"Didn't I tell you to get the hell out?" She glared at Garrett with hatred in her eyes.

"I'm leaving," he said.

"Good. And take all of your shit with you."

"I'm not getting out. Not yet. Not 'til we figure all this out," he told her. There was something strange in his voice.

"No, you said you were leaving, and I want you gone," she told him. "Go be with your baby mama and your other daughter! Go be with Randy! Isn't that who she really is, Garry? All this time, all these years, that's who you've been talking about, your side piece! Miranda my ass—"

"Sylvia, she's dead, okay? She's gone! Yes, Miranda is Randy, but now she's dead. That was the hospital. She died about twenty minutes ago."

And like that, just when Sylvia thought the nightmare couldn't get any worse, it did.

Janelle

"You've reached the voicemail box of—"

Janelle ended the call before the message continued. She had been trying to reach Sylvia for the past two days. It seemed as if her sister was flaking on their afternoon plans, which included manicures, pedicures, shopping at the mall, and dinner.

"She didn't answer?" Nivea, Janelle's friend, asked. They had been waiting in the lobby of the crowded nail boutique for the past fifteen minutes, and Janelle knew they were in jeopardy of missing their appointment.

"Nope," Janelle said.

"Maybe she's on her way," Natalie, Nivea's sister, said.

She sent Sylvia a text, telling her that they were at the salon, then said, "But I ain't waiting. I'm ready." She nodded to the nail technician, and they followed the small Asian lady into the servicing area. Within minutes, their feet were soaking in steaming water, and their backs were being massaged by the luxurious leather chairs. Janelle leaned her head back and relaxed.

It had been a long week, and she needed this. Her boss at the law firm, where she worked as an executive assistant, had been even more of an asshole than usual due to a few of the junior partners deciding to leave without two weeks' notice. Janelle had been his assistant for the last six years and had never seen him this stressed. Normally, she indulged in a leisurely schedule of coming in a little after eight each morning and leaving before five each afternoon, even with her occasional hour and a half lunch break. Now, she was expected to be at work on time and leave a little later each evening, and he even seem irritated when she took an entire hour for lunch. If it weren't for her hefty salary and generous benefits package, she would have found out where the other attorneys had gone and asked if they needed a well-dressed, efficient, competent, experienced employee such as herself to help them out. But Janelle knew her loyalty remained with Mr. Trout. He was a nice guy, and she hoped things would get back to normal soon.

"So, did you and Mr. Wonderful go out last night?" Natalie asked.

"Shut up, girl. We are cool. And stop calling him Mr. Wonderful," Janelle said, cutting her eyes at her friend.

"He must be something. Y'all have been dating for almost six months now. What's the deal?" Nivea asked.

"Six months is not that long," Janelle told them.

"For you, six months is an eternity." Nivea laughed. "You know you rarely date a guy longer than forty-five days. The poor men never stand a chance. I'm actually kind of proud of you."

As much as she hated to admit it, her friends were right. It had been a while since she had dated one man consistently, but that was mainly because Janelle didn't have the patience to deal with most of the bullshit that comes with dating. Most of the guys that approached her were too boring, too broke, too short, too skinny, too many kids, too needy, or simply just too much and she just wasn't attracted to them. Janelle liked a certain type of guy, and unfortunately for her, there weren't that many of her type around. Janelle had pretty much gotten to the point where she was ready to stop dating altogether until she met Jarvis Baldwin six months earlier.

Jarvis was smart, funny, stylish, and charismatic. He was established in his career as a guidance counselor, and Janelle loved how passionate he was about kids. At six foot one, two hundred forty pounds, his frame was perfect to compliment her five foot nine, curvaceous, two hundred–pound body. He was clean cut, well dressed, intelligent, and attractive. To top it off, Jarvis was consistent, and he knew how to plan and execute a date, something most men she met had no knowledge of. Jarvis wasn't clingy, either. They texted one another once or twice a day and only talked maybe once a week. Janelle enjoyed her freedom and peace of mind and hated dealing with men who needed to call or text all day and night. She liked Jarvis and enjoyed spending time with him.

"I think he is wonderful. And he's fine." Natalie shrugged.

"She is right. He is fine," Nivea agreed.

"Since when did you two become the Jarvis Baldwin fan club?" Janelle asked.

"I'm just wondering what the deal is with the two of you," Nivea commented.

"There is no deal. Why does it have to be a deal? We date, we hang out, and we chill, that's it. We're friends."

"So, do you like him?" Natalie asked.

"Of course I like him. Do you think I would be dating him for this long if I didn't like him? Come on. Y'all know me better than that."

"Do you consider him more than just a friend?" Nivea asked.

"Hold on. When you say 'hang out and chill,' does that mean what I think it means?" Natalie asked.

Nivea nodded. "If you think it means they are fucking, then yes."

At the sound of the word *fucking*, all three nail technicians, who had been silently working on their feet, began laughing, confirming what Janelle knew all along: they had been listening to this conversation.

"Why did you say it like that?" Janelle frowned.

"Okay, they are screwing, having sex—"

"We are dating." Janelle interrupted Nivea. "We go bowling, to the movies, dinner. . . ."

"Then you come home and have sex. It's all good. You are grown. It's okay." Nivea laughed.

"If I had a man that fine, I would have sex with him too. That's for damn sure," Natalie told them. "That brother is fine. Morris Chestnut in *The Best Man* fine."

"Wait a sec, Nat. He is good looking, but he ain't that fine," Nivea corrected her.

"Naw, he ain't that fine," Janelle agreed. "He ain't Denzel in *Training Day* fine."

"No, and he definitely ain't Channing Tatum in *Magic Mike* fine either." Natalie laughed.

"Or Alex Rodriguez in *Magic Mike* fine!" Nivea laughed so hard that her foot slipped into the water and it splashed all over the nail tech. The woman shrieked and quickly grabbed a towel, handing it to Nivea.

"Y'all have got issues." Janelle shook her head.

"True, but the point is, for the first time in a very long time, you seem to be happy. And I'm happy for you. But I need for you to keep things in perspective and realize that there will come a point when you are going to have to decide if you want more from this."

Janelle sighed and thought about what her friends were saying, which, oddly enough, was right. Jarvis was a great guy; actually, he was an amazing guy. But even though they had been dating for a while, Janelle wasn't sure if a relationship was something she wanted, let alone if Jarvis wanted one. He didn't bring it up, and neither did she. She was comfortable the way things were.

"I don't know if I'll ever really want anything more than what we have right now." Janelle quickly realized she had spoken the words out loud.

"What the hell are you talking about, Janelle? Isn't that the point of dating? To connect with someone on a deeper level and discover if they are your soul mate and fall in love?" Nivea asked.

"Uhhhh, no." Janelle shook her head. "The purpose of dating is to have some sort of social interaction with the opposite sex so that you get to know one another and discover if you like them well enough that you would be willing to sleep with them."

Nivea and Natalie looked at her like they were abhorred by what she had just said, and so did the nail technicians.

"You're gonna mess this up," Natalie said.

"There is nothing to mess up!" Janelle told her.

"One day, you are truly gonna have to let your guard down and allow yourself to fall in love." Nivea shook her head.

"You act like I've never been in love before," Janelle told her.

"Yeah, that's the problem. You still is." Nivea sighed and sat back in her chair.

Janelle couldn't believe what Nivea was implying. She glanced over at her best friend but didn't say a word. Nivea didn't understand her situation. No one did. But it was her life, and if she was happy being in a noncommittal situation with Jarvis, then that's all that mattered.

Later that night, after several hours of retail therapy and dinner with her friends, Janelle was relaxing on her sofa, flipping through TV channels, when her phone rang.

"I wanna see you." A deep voice greeted her after she answered.

"No."

"Why not? Don't you wanna see me?"

"No."

"Just for a few minutes. Come on, Nelly."

"No."

"I'm coming over to your house."

"No, you're not. Besides, I'm not going to be there. As a matter of fact, I'm not home now."

"You're a liar. I hear the television in the background."

"That doesn't mean I'm at home."

"I'm on my way."

"You're gonna be disappointed. Don't come over here. I mean it."

"Fine, then go where I can see you."

Janelle hung up the phone, threw on a pair of yoga pants, a T-shirt, and sneakers, grabbed her duffel bag, and headed to the 24-hour gym near her home. After putting her belongings into a locker, she stretched for about five minutes. It was one o'clock in the morning, and the gym was pretty empty. She put in her ear buds and climbed on one of the treadmills.

Just as she began walking, a man got on the machine beside her. Janelle walked for a few minutes and then sped her machine up. The man beside her matched her speed and continued to do so each time she did. Finally, after about forty-five minutes, Janelle stopped her machine and climbed off. She walked over to the water fountain, and the man followed. She took a drink of water, turned to him, stared for a second, and finally said, "Stalker."

"Sexy." He smiled.

"What do you want?"

"You."

Janelle walked away, and he followed. The two found seats in the empty, dimly lit area of the gym's closed juice bar.

"How are you?" he asked.

"I'm good. Work's good, the family's good, everything is good." Janelle sighed.

"What about your man Jarred? Is he good?"

"His name is Jarvis, and you know that. And he is good too."

"He may be good, but I'm better, and you know it."

"That's what you think, but I know different." Janelle shrugged. She looked around the gym to see if anyone was watching them.

"Stop being so paranoid."

"I don't have a reason to be paranoid. You do."

"I'm not worried."

"You're not worried about being caught?"

"Caught what? Talking to a friend at the gym? That's all that we're doing. There's nothing wrong with that. But even if I did get 'caught,' as you call it, seeing you makes it well worth it. I love you." He reached over and ran his fingers along her neck and smiled at her.

For a second, Janelle swooned. She knew he loved her, and she loved him too. Love had nothing to do with it, though. They had established their love years ago. She wanted to see him just as much as he wanted to see her, which was why she even came to a place where she knew he would find her. But the fact that he had to sneak and see her at the gym at one o'clock in the morning just confirmed the fact that even being friends was wrong. She reminded herself that she was not Olivia and he was not Fitz, and they were not characters in a Shonda Rhimes television show. She snapped back to reality and stood up.

"Goodbye, Titus."

Sylvia

Sylvia was lying across her bed when she heard the doorbell ring. She sat up and saw that it was after one o'clock in the afternoon and she had slept most of the day away, something she had been doing for nearly a week. It was as if she were in a fog that she couldn't get out of. She knew she had completed her daily routines of taking Peyton to school and picking her up, and even making dinner a few times, but Sylvia couldn't remember the details. All she wanted to do was sleep. It was the only time she didn't feel any type of emotion. When she was awake, she had to deal with anger, hurt, and confusion, especially when Garry, who was the cause of it all, tried calling her. She still hadn't replaced her broken cell phone, and when she ignored his calls to the house phone, he called Peyton's phone and asked to speak with her. She told him time and time again that she needed time to think, but he insisted that they needed to talk this out. Sylvia refused, saying that she had nothing to say. Her life was one huge ball of confusion, and sleep seemed to be the only way she got any peace in her life.

"Hi, Aunt Nelle," she heard Peyton's voice say as the front door opened.

"Hey, sweetie, where is your mom?"

It was Janelle. Sylvia hadn't talked to her sister at all, so she had no clue what was going on. When she heard her voice, she remembered the girls' day she was supposed to have with her yesterday.

"She's in her room. She's not feeling well," Peyton replied.

"Is she okay? What's wrong? Syl, I'm coming up," Janelle called up the stairs.

Sylvia jumped up and ran into the bathroom. She quickly washed her face and brushed her teeth, catching a reflection of herself in the mirror. Her eyes seemed glossed over, but she was glad they were no longer swollen from all the tears she had cried over the past few days. Last night was the first night that she hadn't cried herself to sleep. It was as if she no longer had any more tears inside, just an empty ache inside her chest. She brushed her shoulder-length hair, which was standing all over her head, into a ponytail and wrapped her bathrobe around her. When she came out, Janelle was sitting on her bed, talking to Peyton.

"What's wrong with you?" her sister asked.

"Migraine," Sylvia answered. It wasn't a lie. Her head had been aching for days, right along with her heart.

"I've been calling you. You didn't call or show up yesterday, and then when I didn't see y'all at church, I figured something was wrong. Where is Garry? He didn't come home this weekend?"

Sylvia knew she was going to have to tell her sister what was going on, and she decided to just go ahead and get it over with. "Peyton, go watch TV," she said.

"Yes, ma'am." Peyton looked at her mom and then her aunt, and slowly walked out of the room, closing the door behind her.

"What's going on? What's wrong?" Janelle asked.

"There was an accident last week," Sylvia said.

"An accident? With who? Garry?"

"A woman that Garry knows was in an accident. She . . . she was killed." Sylvia sat on the bed. Her voice was trembling.

"Oh, wow. Did you know her?" Janelle asked.

"No, I didn't know her. I never met her."

"Okay, so what happened? Why are you so upset, Syl?" Janelle moved closer to her.

"This woman and Garry were friends, and he . . ." The tears that Sylvia thought she had no more of suddenly reappeared and began falling. She could feel Janelle's arms around her.

"Sylvia, no," Janelle said. "Please don't tell me this woman and Garry . . ."

Sylvia nodded and collapsed into her sister's arms. Janelle held her close and rocked her, the same way she had when their mother passed away. Although Sylvia was the older sister, Janelle always seemed to be the stronger one emotionally. She was always nonchalant and guarded when it came to love and relationships with anyone.

"Syl, it's okay. Don't cry. I'm so sorry," Janelle told her. "I can't believe this."

"Believe it. It's true."

"And now she's dead?" Janelle asked.

"Yes." Sylvia sat up and wiped her eyes. "But their daughter is alive."

"Whose daughter? What do you mean 'their'?"

"Well, apparently, in addition to his having a mistress, Garry also has a daughter named Jordan that he's never mentioned."

"Shit, this is crazy," Janelle hissed. "Sylvia, what are you gonna do?"

"I don't know. I've been asking myself that same question for the past four days, and I don't have an answer yet," Sylvia sniffed.

"Where is Garry now? What is he saying?"

"I guess he is with his daughter. I haven't really talked to him. I was going to. I mean, I tried, but I guess I was too angry. I didn't want to hear what he had to say."

"How old is his daughter?"

Sylvia couldn't help but laugh because she knew as soon as Janelle heard the answer, her sister would go off. "Fifteen."

"Fifteen? What the hell? How the hell does he have a fifteen-year-old daughter? You all have been married nineteen years."

"I know," Sylvia said.

"Peyton just turned seventeen."

"I know."

"That's a secret he's been keeping for sixteen years. It takes nine months to have a baby! That's a long-ass time to keep a secret!"

"I know."

"Where is—"

Janelle was interrupted by the doorbell ringing. They both listened as Peyton ran down the steps to answer it.

"Who is it, Peyton?" Sylvia called out.

"It's Uncle K," Peyton yelled up the steps.

"Did you tell Kenny?" Janelle asked.

Sylvia shook her head.

Kenneth Bell, Sylvia's business partner, walked into the bedroom. He and Sylvia had been friends for years, attended the same college, and worked for the same public relations firm until they ventured off on their own a few years ago and started their own company, Concepts Unlimited. With Sylvia's creativity and Kenneth's technical abilities, along with their contacts in business and the community, Concepts Unlimited became an instant success. Their clientele was varied and included everything from a premier wine and beverage company to a teenage entrepreneur who had just started his own cologne line.

"You just walk into someone's bedroom without knocking?" Janelle asked.

"What are you doing here?" Sylvia asked, wiping her eyes.

"I came to do something you haven't been doing the past week—work," Kenny said, reaching into the leather bag on his shoulder and pulling out manila folders. "We have a meeting with a new client in the morning. The director of Brittany's Place."

"Shit, I forgot about that too." Sylvia shook her head. The meeting had been scheduled for weeks, and she was supposed to have several ideas ready to discuss with the director and board of trustees of the home for mentally disabled adults.

"I guess that means you haven't worked on any ideas for the fundraising campaign for the hospital either, huh?" Kenny shook his head.

"I'm sorry, Kenny. I have a lot going on right now," Sylvia told him.

"And I don't?" he asked.

"What do you have going on other than juggling your multiple women?" Janelle asked.

"Are you still mad because I won't include you in my rotation, Janelle?"

"Negro, please." Janelle rolled her eyes.

Sylvia couldn't help smiling at the two of them. They always went at it. If she didn't know any better, she would think there was some underlying sexual tension between her friend and business partner and her younger sister. Both had always assured her that nothing was further from the truth.

"Whatever you got going on is gonna have to wait. We got too much work to do," Kenny said, handing her the folders and then pulling out his laptop and opening it.

"What's wrong with you? Don't you see that now is not the time for this?" Janelle asked, "You barged in here while we were having a private, personal conversation like it's nothing."

"Fine. What's going on? Tell me so I can fix it and we can get this work done. What is it now? The florist you were trying to hire for the wedding can't get the orchids you wanted, or is the jazz quartet booked up on that weekend? I get it, this event is major, and I realize that it's a milestone, but this business is my life, and the same way we worked hard to start it is the same way we have to continue to work hard to keep it."

"Kenny," Janelle said. "Hold up—"

"No, Janelle, your sister is becoming consumed with all of this wedding stuff, and the wedding is months away."

"Kenny—"

"Garry and you have—"

"Kenny!"

"What?" Kenny asked.

"You need to stop. As a matter of fact, you need to leave." Janelle stood up.

"Leave?" Kenny was confused.

"He doesn't need to leave." Sylvia shook her head. She knew Kenny meant well and was only trying to motivate her into getting the work done.

"Yes, he does," Janelle told her sister. "He can't just walk in here and talk to you that way. You don't have to take it, either."

"What are you talking about?" Kenny asked. "Your sister knows I'm joking. Well, sort of. I am sick of this damn wedding."

"Well, I have great news for you. There may not even be a wedding," Sylvia announced.

"What? Why?" Kenny frowned.

"Sylvia," Janelle said, leaning over and whispering, "Should you be talking about this to Kenny?"

"Kenny has been my friend and business partner for years. He's going to find out sooner or later, and so is everyone else."

"Find out what?"

"That my husband's mistress was killed in a car crash, but luckily, his teenage daughter survived."

Surprisingly, telling Kenny was easier than she expected. Maybe it was because she had just told Janelle. But saying it this time made it more like fact rather than the fiction that she had been hoping it was. Somehow, it was as if she needed Kenny to know because he had always been real with her and honest. It was one of the qualities that she loved about him, and it made him the ideal person to go into business with.

Sylvia waited for him to say something, anything, to give her some idea as to what she should do. Hoping that whatever Kenny had to say would be the words of wisdom to put this entire ordeal into perspective for her, she waited with bated breath for his response.

After what seemed like the longest pause ever, sadly, the only thing Kenny said was, "Damn, Syl, that's fucked up."

Janelle

"Did you have a nice time?" Jarvis asked as they walked out of the restaurant.

"Of course I did," Janelle said and smiled. "I always do."

"You seemed kind of distracted," he said, taking her by the hand as they walked to his car. It was a nice spring evening, and they had enjoyed an action-packed Leonardo Di Caprio movie before coming to dinner at a well-known local seafood spot.

Although Janelle was having a great time, her mind had drifted to her sister. When she had left Sylvia's home earlier, she and Kenny were working on their latest projects, and Sylvia had assured her that she would be fine. Janelle knew that she would, but she was still worried.

She couldn't believe that Garry, whom she had known for years, had been having an affair. There hadn't been any signs. She thought they were happy, and although she wasn't crazy enough to believe that there was such a thing as a perfect marriage, she thought Sylvia and Garry were damn near close. She had never seen them argue and Sylvia never seemed angry or sad, until now. Janelle kept wondering why he had done it, and how Sylvia could not have known.

"So, you want to go back to my place for a little while?" Jarvis asked her.

She looked up at his dimpled smile and nodded. "Of course I would."

Jarvis leaned over and kissed her softly. Janelle closed her eyes and enjoyed the taste of his mouth on hers. His lips were soft and gentle as he caressed her chin gently. Heat began rising from within her, and she couldn't wait to get to his place. Even her concern for Sylvia and her marriage wasn't enough to distract her from the great sex she knew they would be having as soon as they got to his home.

Once they arrived, Jarvis wasted no time slipping her out of her clothes and leading her into his bedroom. She lay on the bed and wrapped her legs around his body as he kissed her all over, starting with her neck and working his way down, sucking one hardened nipple while playing with the other one. Janelle arched her back and moaned his name as he slipped his finger into her wetness and fingered her clitoris. Soon, his finger was replaced by his tongue, licking and tasting her until she climaxed. He eased his way back up on top of her, and her fingers found their way to his hardness.

She felt along his thick shaft, enjoying the feel of it in her hands, and guided him inside of her. For a few moments, Jarvis didn't move, allowing her to enjoy his being there. He slowly began to go deeper and deeper, following the rhythm of Janet Jackson's "Anytime, Anyplace" that she could hear playing from his nearby speakers. At some point, they shifted, and she got on top, and it was her turn to set the pace. She slowly rode him, staring into his eyes and enjoying the sounds he made as his hands gripped her ass. Her body moved up and down, and she leaned forward to play with his chest. Janelle could feel his body tightening, and she knew it would only be a few more minutes until he exploded within her. She moved faster and faster, rotating her hips in a circular motion and calling his name out as the walls of her hotness tightened with each thrust.

"Ahhhhhh!" Jarvis moaned as he came inside her, and she collapsed on his chest, satisfied.

"You okay?" he asked after a few moments.

"I'm good. You okay?" she asked him.

"Definitely," he said.

They lay there together, listening to the music, until she could hear him snoring softly under her. Janelle slipped from under his arms and into the bathroom, where she quickly washed up and got dressed. When she walked back into the bedroom, he was still sleeping. She kissed him on the forehead and let herself out.

An hour later, she was showered, in her pajamas, and watching television in her own bed when her cell phone rang. She looked and saw that it was Titus. Remembering the dilemma her sister was in, she almost ignored the call, but then figured there was no harm in talking to him on the phone. After all, they were *friends*.

"Hello." She sighed into the phone.

"What are you doing?" he asked.

"Watching TV and about to go to bed."

"How was church?"

"It was good."

"Did you pray for me?"

"Always."

"I know you do. So, what did you do today? Did you and your boo go out tonight?"

"Why?"

"Because I know y'all hang out every weekend, and last night you were with your girls, so I figured y'all would be boo'd up tonight."

Janelle shook her head and confessed, "We went to dinner and a movie."

"Aw, that's so nice. Was it good?"

"The movie or the dinner?"

"Both," he replied. "And the sex."

"I'm getting off this phone," she told him. "Good night, Titus."

"Wait, I'm sorry. Don't hang up. I'm sorry. You know I was just messing with you."

"Whatever."

"Tell me something good," he said, and Janelle couldn't help smiling. When they first started dating, it was how he would start all of their phone conversations late at night. The fact that she was able to talk to him about any and everything was one of the reasons she had fallen in love with him. Titus had the uncanny ability to just listen to her like no one else could.

"I don't know."

"What's wrong, Janelle? Talk to me."

Janelle paused, wondering if she should tell him about Garry and Sylvia. But then she decided not to. Instead, she said, "Nothing. I think I need a vacation, that's all."

"You just went to the Dominican Republic a little while ago."

"That was last summer. I need another getaway."

"You stay getting away, girl. I know your passport is full, and you probably need a new one."

Janelle laughed. She loved to travel, and although she had been to Jamaica, Italy, the Dominican Republic, London, and Greece, there were still a lot of places she wanted to go.

"Don't hate because you can't come with me."

"Ouch, that hurt," he told her. "But you know anywhere with me is paradise."

"You really are ridiculous. You know that, right?"

"Yeah, I do. But why the sudden need to get away? Tell me what's wrong."

"Nothing," Janelle lied.

"I know you better than anyone. Something's wrong. But if you don't wanna talk about it tonight, that's cool. I'm here when you're ready."

"I know you are, but I'm good. Really I am."

"You're better than good; you're amazing. But even amazing people go through stuff. Including you and me."

"Thanks, Titus. Listen, it's late, and I gotta get up early in the morning. I will talk to you later."

"Good night, Nelly. I love you."

Janelle hung the phone up without saying anything else. She looked at the time on her phone and saw that they had been on the phone for longer than she thought. It seemed cliché, but time really did seem to fly whenever she talked to Titus. She wished that she could have that same level of joviality with Jarvis sometimes, but it just wasn't the same. And time had shown her that she would never share that with another man. Titus knew her deepest, darkest secrets, her fears, and her thoughts. He knew how she was feeling without her having to say a word. If only she hadn't made the mistake of letting him go all those years ago, things would be so different. If she hadn't been scared and had followed her heart, they would be together.

She remembered that day as if it were yesterday.

It was her junior year of college, and she had just buried her mother a month before. Janelle stared at the white plastic contraption in her hand with the bright pink plus sign, indicating that she was pregnant. She had only been dating Titus for a few months, and she thought they were being careful each time they had sex. But clearly, they hadn't been careful enough. There was no way she was ready to be a mother. She quickly called a nearby clinic and made an appointment to take care of her unplanned problem the following day.

She didn't tell anyone. Her mother was gone, and Sylvia was still an emotional wreck every time she called her. Janelle didn't want to add any more stress. She thought about telling Titus, but he had gone home for a family emergency himself. Janelle knew he wasn't ready to be a father either. They had both said they wanted to wait until they were in their late thirties and established in their careers before even thinking about being parents. They wanted to live life, have fun, travel, and enjoy one another. A baby was nowhere in the plans. So, Janelle made the decision for both of them. It was the hardest decision of her life, yet the procedure seemed so simple. Within four hours of her arrival, it was over and done. She caught a cab back to the dorm and was in bed resting when her phone rang.

"Janelle, we need to talk," he told her.

Janelle knew something was wrong because he called her by her name. She wondered if somehow he had found out what she had done.

"What's wrong?" she asked.

"You know how much I love you."

"Titus, just tell me what's wrong," she pleaded. "Why did you have to go home?"

"Janelle, Tricia, my ex . . . she had a baby."

"She had a what?"

"She had a baby. A boy. I didn't even know she was pregnant, and neither did my family, until her mom called my house and told my parents she was in labor."

Janelle felt herself becoming nauseated. She didn't know if it was from the anesthesia she had earlier or from the news Titus gave her. Either way, she knew that not only was she going to be sick, but she and Titus were over. He had a baby by his ex, and she had just aborted one.

"Baby, say something," he begged her.

There was nothing Janelle could have said that day. She quickly congratulated him and hung up the phone. For weeks, Titus had tried to contact her. She ignored his calls, so then he sent letters to which she didn't respond. He ended up leaving school, joining the military, and marrying Tricia. In Janelle's mind, it was her punishment for killing the baby that she carried without even telling him.

No man that she dated ever compared to what she'd had with Titus. She never felt anything like what she had felt for him. They didn't speak or see each other for years, until one day, nearly three years ago, she was pumping gas, and she heard a familiar voice behind her.

"Nelly?"

She turned and saw that it was him, a little older and a few pounds heavier. When their eyes met, it was the same electricity that she felt all those years ago when she first met him. He ran up to her and hugged her so tight that he lifted her off the ground. They parked their cars and went into a nearby diner where they had coffee and played catchup. She was telling him about her job at the firm and how much she enjoyed it when her eyes fell onto the small gold band on his left hand.

"I see you're still married," she said softly.

He reached across the table and touched her empty left ring finger and said, "I see you're not."

She shrugged and sat back in the booth across from him. "Nope, I'm not. I am glad things worked out for you and Tricia. Do you have any more kids?"

"No, just the one son, Tarik."

"Tarik, okay. And how old is he?"

"He's thirteen."

"Wow, thirteen," Janelle said. She thought about the decision she'd made, and it made her realize she would be the mother of a twelve-year-old. It seemed like eons ago, not just over a decade.

"Yeah, thirteen long years."

"So, what are you doing here?"

"I . . . well, we've been in the area a little over a year. This is my last duty station before I retire in a few years, so we decided to buy a house in Landville Estates."

"That's crazy. I bought a condo a year ago in Landville Courts."

"We're neighbors." He laughed.

Janelle stared into his handsome face and remembered how much she missed that sound. Again, she looked at his finger and came back to reality. "Well, it was nice catching up with you. I should be going," she told him and stood up.

"Janelle, don't leave. Not yet. Just stay a little while longer, please. I have missed you, missed this, so much. It's like when I lost you all those years ago, I lost a piece of myself. I swear, I think about you all the time, and it's like God finally answered my prayers and allowed me to see you again. Come on. Just one more cup of coffee, please."

Janelle looked into his eyes. As much as she wanted to stay and talk with him, the fact was that he was still married. He said one cup of coffee, but she knew it would have the potential to be so much more.

"I'm sorry, Titus, but I have to go. It was great seeing you. It truly was. I am glad things turned out so well for you."

"Nelly." Titus stood up and touched her arm. "Please, I can't let you go again."

"Titus, don't do this. I have to go," Janelle told him. She gave him a quick hug and kissed his cheek.

"Goodbye."

From that day on, for about three months, Janelle avoided going to the gas station in her neighborhood, fearing that she would run into Titus again. It didn't matter that they had the cheapest gas in town and the best nachos. She couldn't risk it. She didn't know if she would have the willpower to say no if he asked to see her again. Seeing him that one time had opened up a floodgate of emotions that she thought she had locked

*away for good. But now, she constantly thought of him.
It killed her to know that he lived a few streets away,
with his wife and son, of course, but he was still there.
It was as if God was adding insult to injury. Not only
had He not allowed her to meet anyone else and fall in
love after Titus, but out of all of the states, the cities, the
neighborhoods in the world, God had placed Titus and
his happy family right up the street from her.*

*"It's not fair," she said out loud to no one while she was
picking up a bottle of wine from the grocery store late
one Friday night.*

"What's not fair?"

*Janelle dropped the bottle of Moscato she was holding,
and it shattered at her feet.*

*"What the hell are you doing here?" she snapped at
Titus.*

*"Buying some snacks," he told her, holding up a bag of
Doritos and smiling.*

*Janelle looked down at the mess she caused. "Damn
it."*

*"It's okay. I'm sure they have a mop." His eyes twinkled
with amusement as he laughed. "Not that you know how
to use it. You always sucked at housework."*

*"Shut up," she said and walked away, Titus right on
her heels. "Excuse me. I dropped a bottle in aisle seven,"
she told the cashier.*

*"Pete, clean up on aisle seven," the woman said into
the microphone then looked at Titus and said, "Are you
ready to check out? We close in five minutes."*

*Janelle walked off, and he said, "Not yet. We'll be right
back."*

"Why are you following me?"

"Why are you running away from me?"

*"I'm not. I'm going to get my bottle of wine to replace
the one that you made me drop," she told him. She*

walked down the aisle and grabbed an even bigger bottle of Moscato, thinking that it was going to take more wine than she'd anticipated after seeing him.

"Nelly, come on. Don't do this."

"Don't do what?" Janelle asked. "What do you want from me?"

"I want you to talk to me," he told her. "I want you to stop acting like I got the plague. I want you to stop tripping."

"Fine." Janelle stopped in the middle of the aisle. "Hello, Titus, how are you? How's your wife and kid?"

Titus shook his head at her. "You're trying to be funny."

"I'm not. You want me to talk to you, so I'm talking. How are you enjoying this weather? Hot enough for you? What about those Lakers? Kobe is having a helluva season, isn't he? Have you seen the new—"

Suddenly, Titus's mouth was on hers, and she found herself lost in his kiss. She literally lost her breath, and without warning, she dropped the second bottle of wine. The sound of it crashing to the floor gave her a reason to pull away from him.

She turned and faced the lanky teenager who had just finished cleaning up the mess she caused previously and said, "I'm sorry."

He smiled, winked at her, and said, "It's all good."

"We'll pay for both bottles," Titus assured him.

Titus reached on the shelf and passed Janelle another bottle and asked, "Did you need me to carry this to the front for you?"

Janelle snatched it from him and walked away without saying a word. She got to the register, bottle in tow, and told the cashier to ring up all three bottles of wine. Just as she reached into her purse for her check card, Titus reached across her and paid.

"You don't have to do that," Janelle told him.

"Well, technically, I do," he said. "Especially since I was the reason you dropped the other two."

"You have a point." Janelle apologized to the cashier again, grabbed her bag, and rushed to her car.

"Nelly! Janelle!" Titus called behind her.

She got to her car, unlocked and opened the door, and got in. Just as she was about to close the door, she felt him grab it.

"Titus, please just go," she pleaded with him.

"Fine, I'll go. After you give me your number," he said. "I promise. Give it to me and I'll go."

"Give you my number for what? What sense does that make?"

"So that I can call you, check on you, and make sure you're okay. And it makes sense because you're my friend. I care about you. I lo—"

"Stop it, please. I'm not giving you my number. Your friend? Friends don't do what we just did in the aisle of the store. You're married, for God's sake. Anybody could have seen that shit!"

"I know, and I'm sorry about that. I couldn't resist. I promise it won't happen again. But I don't regret it. It felt good and it felt right, and you know it."

Kissing Titus did feel good, but the fact still remained that he was married, and Janelle didn't do married men. Even if it was Titus.

"I'm not giving you my number. Now, please get out of my way," Janelle said, slamming the car door shut. She started the engine and pulled off so fast, Titus barely had a chance to get out of the way.

For days afterwards, she thought about the kiss and wondered if she should have given him her number. Maybe he was right; there was nothing wrong in their being friends. It wasn't as if she planned on sleeping *with him. She pondered and wondered, thinking about him constantly. Then late one night, she got a random friend request from some guy named "Ty Boogie," which also happened to be the pet name she'd had for him. Instead of hitting delete, Janelle accepted the request.*

Now, three years later, she and Titus were friends.

Sylvia

"Where's Garry now?" Kenny asked later as Sylvia walked him to the door after they finished the proposals.

"He's off making final resting plans for his side chick, I guess," Sylvia told him. She could see Kenny trying not to laugh, but even she couldn't help smiling at her comment.

"You know you're gonna have to tell Peyton. She's a bright kid and knows something is going on. She's worried about you."

Sylvia knew he was right. Although she hadn't said anything, she knew her child was confused by her behavior recently, starting with her announcement that her father wouldn't be home for a while. Sylvia didn't give her a specific explanation, just that he wasn't coming home anytime soon.

"Why should I be the one to tell her? Garry is the one who's been screwing around on us and hiding his other family. Shouldn't he be the one to confess his indiscretions? I haven't done anything wrong."

"It doesn't matter who tells her, but someone needs to. As a matter of fact, it would probably be best if both her mother *and* father talk to her. This doesn't just affect the two of you; it affects the entire family."

"I can't believe Garry would do this to us. I hope Miranda . . . Randy . . . whoever she is was worth losing his family over."

"So, it's over? I thought you hadn't made your decision."

"Yes, it's over. The man had a child with another woman years ago that he hid from me. The only reason I found out was because his mistress is dead. Who in their right mind would stay with him? Why should I?"

"Well, because he's your husband and you still love him," Kenny told her.

"What? People would think I was crazy!"

"Wait, wait, wait, calm the hell down and listen. First of all, this is definitely not a decision to be made based on what people think. That's stupid. You shouldn't give a damn about what people would think. Now, listen, I ain't telling you what to do with your marriage. It's definitely not for me to say. What I am telling you is that you need to think things through before you make a decision. You said yourself that you haven't talked to Garry. What you should've probably done was go to church today and prayed about it."

"Shut up, Kenny. I can't talk to him. Every time I hear his voice, I get so fucking *mad*! I didn't do anything to deserve this, and you know it, Kenny. I am . . . was a good wife. He couldn't have found a better woman than me." Sylvia was angry all over again—angry at Garry for what he'd done, and angry at herself for not even realizing what had been going on. *Sixteen years.* Sixteen years he'd had a mistress, and she'd been too stupid to even know about her. Was she that gullible, or was Garry that good of a liar?

"Who said he did? And you should be telling him all of this."

"I don't even know when he's coming home, Kenny." Sylvia sighed.

"Um, he's pulling into the driveway right now," Kenny told her.

Sylvia looked out of the cracked door and saw Garry's Honda pulling into the driveway beside Kenny's Infinity truck.

"Shit." Sylvia sighed heavily. Suddenly her stomach was full of butterflies, and her heart was pounding. She grabbed Kenny by the arm and said, "Don't go. I need you here to protect me."

"Sylvia, I've known Garry almost as long as I've known you. He doesn't seem like the type that's gonna put his hands on you, and if he has, you've never mentioned it."

"Okay, fine. Maybe *he* is the one who needs you here to protect *him*."

"You're crazy. I'm outta here." Kenny snatched away from her. "Think things through, talk to your husband, and talk to your child. I will see you in the morning. Nine thirty sharp."

Kenny slipped out the door, and she watched him from the window as he walked over and slapped palms with Garry. The two men talked for a few minutes. Sylvia tried to read their lips and even their facial expressions so that she could get an idea of what they were saying, but she was too far. Anxious, Sylvia ran upstairs and into her bedroom. She paced back and forth, taking Kenny's advice and praying that somehow God would help her.

"Daddyyyyyyyy!"

She heard Peyton squeal and run down the stairs.

"Hey, baby," Garry's voice cried out. Sylvia could picture him lifting Peyton off the ground and swinging her around as he always did when he came home. The relationship Garry and Peyton had reminded Sylvia of the one she shared with her own father. The bond between both fathers and daughters was one that was unbreakable. For a second, Sylvia was happy that he was home, until she remembered that Garry had another daughter to bond with. Feelings of betrayal and hurt came flooding over her. She closed the bedroom door and sat on the side of her bed.

"Sylvia." There was a knock at the door.

"What, Garry?" Sylvia snapped.

The door eased open, and he walked into the room. Sylvia pretended to be looking at the folders that were still on the bed where she and Kenny had been working.

"How are you?"

"Please don't try and patronize me to feel me out, Garry. I'm still pissed, I'm still hurt, and I still don't want to talk to you. That's how I am. Next question."

"Sylvia, I know you're pissed and hurt. I don't blame you—"

"Why would you blame me? I'm not the one who's been cheating for the past sixteen years, so I guess I'm blameless in this situation. Can you say the same thing?"

"I haven't been cheating for the past sixteen years, Sylvia. I swear."

"Well, you have a fifteen-year-old daughter, and your mistress carried a baby for nine months, so that's damn near sixteen years." Sylvia stood up and hissed, "Can you explain that?"

"I did sleep with Randy a long time ago. It wasn't an affair; it was a mistake. The mistake resulted in Jordan." He walked over and tried to touch her, but she pulled away from him.

"Stop saying it was a mistake like you accidentally washed a black sock in the white clothes, or you forgot to tell them no tomatoes on the burger you got me. It's bigger than a fucking mistake. You had a whore on the side. That's not a mistake."

"She isn't—wasn't a whore. It wasn't like that."

"And now you're gonna stand there and defend her? To me?"

"No, I'm not. . . . Sylvia, listen to me. If you just let me explain—"

"The person you need to explain this to is your daughter, who has been worried sick about you."

"Why? What did you tell her?"

"I didn't tell her anything. That's not my place."

"You're right. It's my place—"

"No, it's *our* place to tell her. This doesn't just affect you or me. It affects *us*! Peyton!" Sylvia called her daughter's name.

"Yes, Mom?"

"Come in here!"

"Sylvia, I don't think—" Garry told her.

"No, Garry, it's obvious you *don't* think. You didn't think all those years ago when you decided to sleep with your *friend*. But unlike you, I'm not hiding any of this from *our* daughter."

The door opened, and Peyton walked in and looked at her parents. There was a look of fear on her face that Sylvia only saw when she took her daughter to the doctor. She knew something was up, and whatever it was, it wasn't good.

"Peyton, we need to talk to you, sweetie. Come and sit down," Sylvia said as she patted the side of the bed and beckoned for her.

Peyton took a seat beside her mother and began to cry.

"Baby, what's wrong?" Garry said, sitting on the other side of their daughter.

"Are you sick?" Peyton asked her father. "Do you have cancer?"

"Why would you think that?" Sylvia asked.

"Because you keep crying, and you said Daddy wouldn't be home for a while. And Aunt Lynne came over and Aunt Nelle and Uncle K, and you all have been so secretive. I heard y'all talking about the hospital and a funeral." Peyton's face was full of worry, and her voice cracked as she spoke.

"Peyton, baby, your father is fine. But we do need to talk to you about something very serious," Sylvia told her.

The last thing she wanted to do was cause Peyton any kind of pain or stress, but she knew this situation wasn't one that they were going to be able to keep a secret. She reached out and rubbed Peyton's back and said, "Your father will explain."

Garry gave Sylvia a slight frown that she quickly ignored. She knew she was putting him on the spot and he probably wasn't expecting to have this conversation with Peyton at this moment, but she didn't care. He had caused this mess, so it was his responsibility to explain it, not hers.

He cleared his throat and finally spoke. "Baby girl, um, the reason we were talking about a hospital is because a woman I know, a . . . friend of mine and her daughter were in a car accident."

"Oh, no! Daddy, that's terrible." Peyton gasped.

"Yeah, it is." Garry nodded.

"Are they okay?" Peyton asked.

"Well, yes and no. My uh, friend . . ." Garry's voice became faint as he spoke. "She died."

"That's sad, Daddy. I'm sorry." Peyton hugged her father.

He looked over at Sylvia in an effort to get her to contribute to the difficult conversation, but she only gestured for him to keep going.

"Um, baby, there's something else." He lifted Peyton's head and stared at her.

"Jordan . . . my friend's daughter . . . she . . . I'm . . . um . . ." He looked over to Sylvia for help, but she rolled her eyes, letting him know that he was going to have to say it himself. "She is my daughter. She's your sister."

"What? How?" Peyton pulled away from her father and looked at Sylvia.

"It's a long story," Sylvia said, deciding that this was enough information for Peyton to digest right now. "And we don't need to get into that part right now. We just feel that you needed to know about what's going on."

"How old is she?"

"She's fifteen," Garry told her.

Peyton looked at Sylvia in disbelief, and Sylvia nodded, letting her know that it was true. The tension in the room instantly became overwhelming. Sylvia could tell that Peyton's emotions matched her own: pain, confusion, anger, and shock. She wondered if telling her had been a selfish move.

"I'm sorry, baby. I messed up big time. I know I did. But I'm going to do any and everything to make it up to you and your mother. I promise I will."

"Are you all getting a divorce?" Peyton asked.

"No!" Garry's voice was so loud that Sylvia and Peyton jumped. "We aren't getting a divorce. I love your mother, and she loves me. I *am not* losing my family and everything we've worked so hard to build. We will get through this."

Garry reached around Peyton and touched Sylvia's shoulder. She flinched slightly, but oddly enough, she didn't snatch away as she'd done the past couple of times he'd touched her. Maybe she was beginning to process everything, and even though she still hurt, it didn't sting as it had a couple of days earlier.

Her eyes remained on her bedroom floor. She wondered if Garry was right. Was this one indiscretion worth losing all that they had? Had it only been one indiscretion, or were there more of "Garry's kids" floating around that she didn't know about?

"So, you have a fifteen-year-old daughter who is in the hospital, whose mother just died? What's gonna happen to her now?" Peyton asked.

"She is scheduled to be released from the hospital in a few days, in time for the funeral. She doesn't have any other family. It was just her and her mom."

Peyton looked from her father to her mother, then back to her father. "So, where is she going to go?"

Garry shrugged slightly and said, "I guess that's what I'm gonna have to figure out."

Janelle

"Lemme get a frozen margarita with sugar, not salt," Janelle told the bartender. The club was packed, as it normally was for First Fridays, and she and Nivea were sitting at the bar, enjoying the scene. Looking across the bar, she saw Kenny walk in, and she waved.

"He is so fine," Nivea whispered.

"If you say so." Janelle laughed.

Kenny was a nice-looking guy. He was tall with a slender build, skin the color of dark chocolate, and a smooth bald head. Born and raised in North Carolina, Kenny still talked with a Southern drawl and used it as part of his charm to attract women, which he had plenty of. The fact that Nivea was gushing over him came as no surprise to her. Janelle had to admit he looked nice in the blue Polo shirt and jeans he wore.

"OMG, he's coming over here!" Nivea squealed.

"What's up, ladies?" Kenny said, hugging them both.

"Hey, Kenny," Janelle said.

"Hi." Nivea smiled.

"You're looking sexy as ever, Nivea. When are you gonna let me take you out?"

"You know that means when are you gonna let him *hit that*, right?" Janelle leaned over and said.

"Stop hating, Nelle. I'm sure you don't believe that, do you?"

"Of course not," Nivea told him. "I know better than that."

"I also hope you know that he is a man-whore." Janelle laughed.

"Whoa, how you gonna call me that?" Kenny pretended he was appalled by what Janelle said.

"The truth hurts, huh?" Janelle laughed. The bartender put her drink in front of her, and before she could touch it, Kenny picked it up and took a sip.

"What the hell? You need to be paying for that too, asshole."

"Again, why I gotta be all that?"

"Do real men even drink margaritas? I didn't think you were the 'fruity drink' type, Kenny." Janelle winked.

"Girl, please, you know ain't nothing fruity about me. Don't even try it. Ask your girl." He pointed in Nivea's direction.

"Whoa, whoa, whoa! Now, *that* I don't know nothing about," Nivea corrected him.

"Yet," Kenny said. "Give me a couple more minutes."

"You are such a jerk," Janelle said.

They ordered another round of drinks, making sure they were on Kenny's tab. A few minutes later, Janelle noticed another woman at the end of the bar staring in their direction.

"Do you know her?"

Kenny looked over to see who Janelle was talking about. He smiled at the woman, who smiled back at him. "Not yet I don't," he said then told the bartender to send a drink over to her.

"You are such a pig. How are you gonna try and holler at my girl while buying another chick a drink? Who does that?"

"Is your friend gonna give me some ass tonight?" Kenny asked.

"Ewwww, no!" Janelle told him.

"That woman down there probably will." Kenny smiled and walked away.

"Where is he going?" Nivea whined, peeking through the crowd.

"Who cares? Again, he's a man-whore," Janelle told her. She reached into her purse and took out her phone. She had texted Jarvis earlier to see if he would be up for company later, but he hadn't responded.

"Aren't all men?" Nivea asked.

"You do have a point." Janelle laughed. "Where's Natalie? Isn't she supposed to be here?"

"She has to work until eleven. Hey, isn't that Jarvis?"

Janelle looked up, and sure enough, Jarvis was walking through the crowd, surrounded by three women.

"Yeah, it is."

"Did you know he was gonna be here?"

"Nope."

"Are you gonna go over there and say something?"

"Nope, why? He's not my man. He can go wherever he wants to with whomever he wants to," Janelle told her. She finished her second margarita and ordered another one. "Can I get a double shot in this one?" At least now she knew why Jarvis hadn't responded to her message. He was too busy being entertained by someone else.

"Hey, isn't that your boy over there?" Kenny walked over and asked. "Jamie?"

"Jarvis," Janelle corrected him. "And yeah, that's him."

"Are you gonna speak to him?"

"I asked that same question," Nivea told him.

Janelle cut her eyes at her friend and said, "Nope, no need."

"Why not? I thought Sylvia said y'all were a thing." Kenny leaned back on the bar.

"No, we're not a thing. We're just cool."

"They just hang out, meaning she's letting him *hit that*." Nivea giggled.

As if he could sense them, Janelle looked over and saw Jarvis looking at them. She smiled and raised her glass. Jarvis walked over and gave her a hug, then kissed her cheek.

"Hey, Janelle, I didn't expect to see you here," he told her.

Janelle inhaled his scent, and he smelled divine. "I can say the same thing." She shrugged and smiled.

"Yeah, it was a last-minute thing. It's one of my cowork-ers' birthday, and we came out to have a few drinks to celebrate."

"You remember my friend Nivea and my sister's busi-ness partner, Kenny." Janelle smiled.

"Hey, how are you guys?" Jarvis nodded.

They made small talk for a few minutes until the shortest of the three women that Jarvis was with walked over and grabbed his arm.

"Jarvis, can you get another round while you're over here? Our waitress is slow."

Janelle looked the woman up and down. She was an average build with an asymmetric haircut. There was nothing really special about her other than the glasses on her face, which Janelle thought were cute. Compared to Janelle, who was wearing fitted jeans, red corset-style top, and stiletto pumps, the lady seemed casual in the simple black shirt and pants she wore.

"Huh? Oh, yeah. No problem. Um, Janelle, this is Sade. She's the IT specialist at our school." Jarvis introduced her.

"Nice to meet you," Janelle said.

"Same here," Sade said. An Usher song began blasting from the speakers, and she pulled Jarvis away, saying, "I love this song. The drinks can wait. *We have* to dance."

Jarvis gave Janelle an uncomfortable look, and she just smirked as he went with Sade onto the dance floor. Janelle turned back around to the bar.

"Wow, that wasn't as awkward as I thought it was gonna be," Kenny commented.

"Why would you think it was gonna be awkward?" Janelle frowned at him.

"Because he's smashing you, and by the other chick's behavior, he's smashing her too," Kenny said. "Well, I take that back. He may not be, but he could if he wanted to, because she would give him some ass in a Mississippi minute."

"And how is a Mississippi minute different from um, let's say, a Tennessee minute? Please tell me." Janelle laughed.

"It's way faster. If it makes you feel any better, she would probably let me smash too if I wanted her," Kenny told her.

"You think any female would let you smash, Kenny."

"Not true. I know you wouldn't."

"I'm glad you realize that." Janelle shook her head. "Because you are so right. But I don't care if he's smashing her. He's not my man. He can do what he wants to, and so can I."

"Then why are you mad?" Kenny asked.

"I would be mad too," Nivea said. "That's an asshole move."

"I'm not mad," Janelle told him.

"You a damn lie, and you ain't gotta lie to me. How long have you been letting him smash?" Kenny asked.

"Six months," Nivea answered.

"Yeah, you mad," Kenny said, still watching Jarvis and Sade on the dance floor. "You wanna dance and make him mad?"

"No, I don't," Janelle told him.

"I do." Nivea hopped off the barstool.

"I bet you do." Kenny laughed then turned to Janelle and said, "You sure you don't wanna join us? I can handle both of y'all."

"I'm sure," Janelle told him.

She watched as her friends went onto the dance floor next to Jarvis and Sade, who were swaying to the music. Again, her eyes met Jarvis's, and she forced a smile. Sade reached and pulled his head down so that she could say something to him. Janelle ordered another drink. She knew her limit was normally three, but she needed another one. She was telling the truth when she said that she wasn't mad about Jarvis being at the club with another chick. What she was feeling wasn't anger; it was disappointment. She had actually thought that maybe there could be something between her and Jarvis. Now, once again, she was wrong. If she did have any feelings for Jarvis, they were now gone. She hoped he and Sade would be happy together.

Janelle reached into her purse and took out her phone. There was one person she knew she loved and who loved her back. She typed the words I Love You into a text message and sent it. Within minutes, she received a message back confirming, I love you too, Nelly. She smiled and decided that it wasn't another drink that she needed at all. The only thing she needed was to see Titus.

Sylvia

"Baby, are you sure you're okay?" Sylvia asked as she sat in traffic. Any other time, she would've been stressed and worried that Peyton would be late for school. Instead, she was grateful for the temporary pause, and she took it as an opportunity to talk. Peyton really hadn't said much about her father's recent revelation. Both she and Garry had made it clear that his transgression had nothing to do with her, and they wanted her to know that they were both there for her. She and Peyton had always had a fairly open relationship, and they talked about everything from sex, drugs, and dating to college, fashion, and current events.

"Mom, please stop asking me that. Are *you* okay?" Peyton raised an eyebrow and asked.

Sylvia took a sip of coffee from the silver travel mug she was holding. "Don't try and deflect, Peyton."

"I'm not the one deflecting. You just keep asking me the same question over and over."

"Fine, let's start over." Sylvia relented and decided to try another approach. "How are you feeling today, Peyton?"

"Oh my God, that's the same thing just worded differently," Peyton whined in exasperation and leaned her head against the car window.

"Peyton."

"Mom."

"I'm trying here."

"I know you are, but you want me to do all of the talking, but you don't wanna talk."

"What does that even mean?"

"It means that you want me to be all open and share my feeling about all of this that's going on, but you don't want to open up and share with me," Peyton said.

The car in front of Sylvia's eased up, and Sylvia followed suit, now hoping that traffic would move faster. But they only moved about a car length ahead and came to a complete stop once again.

"There must be a major accident somewhere," Sylvia said, reaching for the radio button and turning up the volume.

"Nope, that's not gonna work either." Peyton turned the volume back down and said, "You wanted to talk, so we're gonna talk.

"Okay, I have no problem talking," Sylvia told her.

"Good, so, how are you feeling, Mom?" Peyton was now turned toward her.

Sylvia sighed and said, "I'm fine. Worried about you, but I'm fine."

"You can't possibly be fine, Mom. You can be a lot of things, and you can be worried about me, but what you can't be is fine. No way. You're not fine."

"Touché."

"So, I'll ask you again. How are you feeling?"

Sylvia stared at her beautiful daughter, the perfect combination of both her and her husband. "I'm coping, Peyton. Honestly, that's the only way to describe it."

"Coping." Peyton nodded slowly. "I get that."

"You do?" Sylvia asked, wondering if Peyton really understood or if she was saying it to be supportive.

"I do. It's kinda like my Calculus class. I hate it. It's stressful, confusing, difficult, and I struggle, but I press through every day because it's important."

The last thing Sylvia would have compared her current life situation to would be a Calculus class, but in a way, it did make sense. For the past week, she had woken daily, stressed and confused, and it was a struggle, but she pressed her way through because her daughter was important. And despite the turmoil, her family, which included her husband, was still important.

"That's an equitable comparison," Sylvia told her.

"Equitable? Really, Mom? You sound as boring as Dr. Khan." Peyton shook her head and stated, "But I'm glad I got the analogy right."

"You did. And now that you know how I'm doing, you can tell me how you're doing," Sylvia told her.

"I'm doing the same as you, I guess. I'm coping. I am so mad at Daddy for doing this to you, to us. Like, how? Why?"

Sylvia was tempted to tell her that those were the same questions she'd been asking herself, but she didn't. She just let Peyton continue to talk.

"And we're not the only ones he's done this to," Peyton said.

"What do you mean?" Sylvia frowned, wondering if Peyton had somehow found out about another secret family Garry had that she didn't know about.

"The girl, his other . . . uh, daughter. Can you imagine how she's feeling right now? Did she know Daddy had a wife and daughter somewhere? Or were they just as clueless as we were? And now her mother's dead and gone. She has no one and nowhere to go. Daddy was living a double life, pretty much. How am I feeling? I feel like I'm living in a Lifetime movie, for real."

"I wouldn't go that far, but I get what you're saying." Sylvia smiled slightly.

"And I'm mad at myself."

"Yourself? Baby, why? There's no reason for you to be mad at yourself. You haven't done anything wrong. Your daddy and I told you that." Sylvia touched Peyton's arm.

"I'm mad at myself because I feel sorry for Daddy because he's so sad and dealing with all of this, and the last thing he deserves is my sympathy. Why should I feel sorry for him? He's a cheater. He cheated on *you*, and you're the best thing that ever happened to him—his words, not mine."

"Don't be mad at yourself, Peyton. Despite all of this, he's still your dad, and you love him. That's why you feel sorry for him," Sylvia said. "It's fine."

"Do you feel bad for him? Or are you mad at him?"

Again, the traffic began moving, and Sylvia eased along the highway, pausing before speaking. She was livid with her husband, and even though he brought this entire situation on himself, she hated to see the stress and grief he was dealing with. "Both, I guess."

"Who does that to people they love? This is just . . . unforgivable."

Sylvia saw Peyton looking out of the corner of her eye, and she asked, "Is that a question or a statement?"

"I guess it's a question."

"Then I don't really have an answer to it right now," Sylvia told her.

"I understand. But I can't stop thinking about her."

Even though she understood exactly what Peyton meant, the last thing Sylvia wanted her daughter to be thinking about was Garry's mistress, dead or alive. She was grateful that they were finally talking about the situation and she had opened up. It was time to bring this conversation to a close.

"Peyton, you don't—"

"I mean, she's gotta be just as confused as we are, huh?"

"Who?" Sylvia asked.

"Dad's other daughter. It's sad. At least I have you to talk about it with, but she doesn't because her mother is . . . dead. Is Dad going to stay with her?"

"I don't know, Peyton." Sylvia sighed, slightly relieved that she had assumed incorrectly. It was not Miranda that Peyton had been concerned with, but her daughter.

"Mom, is he going to bring her to our house?"

"I highly doubt it." Sylvia shook her head.

"But what if he does? Are you going to let him? I wouldn't be mad at you if you said no, Mom. That's a lot for anyone to deal with, and you're already dealing with a lot right now," Peyton said.

"We're all dealing with a lot right now, but I don't think that's going to happen."

"But what if it does? He already said she has no other family other than him. What if our house is the only other option? What then?"

"Then we'll have to decide as a family. It will have to be a family discussion," Sylvia told her, then said, "Finally, the traffic is moving."

"Can we stop and get coffee? I'm already going to be late, so it won't matter."

"It will matter. Stopping for coffee will make you even later."

"Please, Mom. I need caffeine to help me take the edge off. You know I'm dealing with a lot right now."

"Don't even try it, sis. It ain't gonna work." Sylvia laughed.

A few minutes later, they pulled in front of Peyton's school. Most of the students had already gone inside, but there were still quite a few late arrivals. "You're not the only late one, so they shouldn't say anything. But if they do, just call the house phone," Sylvia said, remembering her cell phone was broken.

"It's no big deal. I'm sure they won't say anything. I'm never late. Oh, look. There's Treva, and she has Starbucks." Peyton waved at another young lady walking toward the car carrying a Starbucks cup.

"Bye, Peyton. See ya, love ya, bye."

Peyton gave her a quick kiss. "Bye, Mom. See ya, love—" Then, Peyton stopped mid-sentence and looked like she was going to cry.

"What's wrong?" Sylvia asked.

"I'm just lucky. I can still kiss you and tell you goodbye. She can't."

Sylvia hugged Peyton tight, grateful for the opportunity to do so. "I love you too, baby."

Peyton got out of the car and turned around. "I know you, Mom, and I support you. So while you're coping, whatever you decide, I got your back no matter what. One thing about it, you always do the right thing, even when it's hard. And whether we like it or not, she's family."

"Syl?"

Sylvia looked up from the proposal she was working on to see Garry standing in the doorway of her office. He looked as if he'd been run over by a truck and for a second, she felt bad for him. Then she remembered what he'd done. Her thoughts went back to the conversation she'd had in the car with Peyton. Despite everything he'd done, she still loved him, and it was normal to have sympathy because she knew he was hurting. But she was still angry and hurt.

Instead of saying anything, she just stared and gave him a slight shrug. He must've taken it as an invitation to come in, because he walked over to her desk.

"I just wanted to talk for a few minutes before I uh, left."

Again, Sylvia stared at him, saying nothing.

"I know you're sick of me saying this, but I'm sorry. You've gotta believe me. I truly am."

She rolled her eyes at him and said, "I know you are, Garry. So please stop saying it."

He looked relieved that she'd spoken. "It's just . . . and I know this is going to sound selfish, but I need you, Syl. I'm going through hell, and I'm at the end of my rope. I'm trying here."

Hearing him say that he was at the end of his rope caused her heart to tear even more. "The end of my rope" was the phrase they used when life came at them too fast and they needed a different kind of support from one another—not just the typical "I'm having a bad day and need to vent," or "I need a hug from my spouse right now" kind of support. It was a cry for help. The times they'd used it had been few and far between.

The first time she'd said it was shortly after both her parents died, Janelle's tuition for her senior year was due, and Sylvia wasn't working. Life came barreling at her all at once, and she felt as if she might lose her mind. Garry called one day and asked how things were going, and that was her response. He became the knot that she held onto until she found the strength to hold herself and eventually climb back up the rope. Garry had always been her knot when she was at the end of her rope, and now he needed her to be his. The question was, could she?

"Garry, I know this isn't easy for you," she muttered.

"It's not, Syl. I want to do the right thing—for everyone, especially you and Peyton. Y'all are my everything. But I also . . ." His voice drifted, and he looked down at the floor.

Sylvia exhaled slowly and asked, "How is she?"

Garry's eyes quickly met hers, and he said, "She's sad and scared and confused."

"Sounds exactly how Peyton is feeling these days."

"But Peyton has her mother."

"Don't do that, Garry. Don't try and guilt me into feeling bad," Sylvia warned.

"I'm not trying to do that, Syl, I swear. Besides, you haven't done anything to feel guilty about."

"What do you want from me, Garry? Just tell me."

"I've made the funeral arrangements, and Jordan is being released in a couple of days, hopefully. I need to know—"

"Garry," Sylvia said before he could even finish his sentence. Her thoughts went to her earlier conversation with Peyton and the question her daughter had asked. Had Garry mentioned something to her about the girl coming to stay with them, or was Peyton just that intuitive?

"It would just be temporary, until I figure everything else out, Syl. She has nowhere else to go except with me. I know it's a lot to ask, but I want to be home, here with you and Peyton. If I'm not here, then there's no way we're going to be able to get through this," Garry said.

"Do you really think we're going to be able to get through it, Garry?" Sylvia asked. It was a question she'd been asking herself over and over, and she still didn't have an answer.

"I do." Garry nodded his head.

"How do you know? Because I damn sure don't."

"I know because I love you, and I'm going to fight for you and our marriage and our family. I know because you're my wife and my best friend, and I'm going to do whatever I have to do to make sure we get through it. Counseling, therapy, whatever you need for me to do, I'll do it."

"Garry, this isn't as simple as—"

"I'm not saying it's simple by any means, Syl. I'm saying it's attainable—by any means necessary."

"I was thinking maybe we would separate until you figure all of this out, and now you're talking about bringing your outside child into our home," Sylvia told him.

Garry flinched slightly, and she knew her words hurt him, but she didn't care. She'd been hurting since that day in the parking lot when he told her who Miranda was.

"Separating? You want a separation?" He looked at her as if he couldn't believe what she had just said.

Until the words escaped her mouth, she hadn't really considered separation. She thought about divorce or remaining together, but separation seemed to make sense because it was normally what people did while they were divorcing. It was the first step, she thought.

Are we divorcing? Do I really want a divorce?

"I, uh, I don't know," Sylvia said.

Garry took another step toward her desk. "We aren't separating, Syl. We still love one another. I love you and you love me. That hasn't changed. We will get through this. I believe that. I need you, Syl. I hate to say it, but it's the truth. I probably sound like a total asshole for saying it, and I know I fucked up. I'm begging."

Tears now fell from Garry's tired eyes and rolled down his cheeks. His beard, which was usually nicely neat and trimmed, was now scruff and scraggly, and he was in dire need of a haircut. He looked like he hadn't eaten or slept in days. Sylvia had never seen her husband so lost and forlorn, and despite her anger and confusion, she was now concerned about Garry's health and overall well-being. He was in no condition to take care of a teenager who'd just lost her mother. Hell, he was falling apart and was barely taking care of himself. She still cared about him, and she knew she had to do the right thing, which was why she closed her eyes and said, "Fine, Garry, whatever. Bring her here—just until you figure this shit out."

"Thank you, Syl," Garry whispered and gave her a slight smile that she didn't return.

"Temporarily, Garry. This isn't going to be permanent. That's not fair to me nor Peyton."

"I understand what you're saying, Sylvia. I appreciate you." He slowly turned and walked out of the office.

Sylvia leaned back and closed her eyes, praying that she wasn't making a mistake. She had to be one of the craziest women on earth to be doing this. Peyton was right. She always felt the need to do the right thing, even if it was hard. She should have probably been a social worker because she had a heart of gold.

Her eyes landed on the corner of a small, yellow piece of paper hiding under the keyboard of her computer. It was the receipt for the Save the Date cards for their vow renewal. Now, here she was wondering if they were even going to make it to their anniversary.

Janelle

"Aunt Nelle?"

"Peyton?" Janelle sat up on her sofa. She didn't even realize she'd fallen asleep until her cell phone rang. Looking at her watch, she saw that it was after eleven. "What's wrong?"

"Nothing's wrong. Well, not really. I just needed to talk."

Janelle could only imagine how her niece was feeling. Peyton and Garry had a wonderful relationship, and her father could do no wrong in her eyes. This had to be weighing heavily on her. The one man she loved more than anything and could depend on had perpetrated the ultimate betrayal on the one woman on earth that she loved more than anything.

"Well, I'm here to listen. You already know that," Janelle told her. "How are you holding up?"

"I'm not. I'm trying, but I'm not."

"Hey, it's okay that you're not, P. No one expects you to be a hundred percent okay. Hell, I'm surprised you're not in shock. This was major, and what your fa—" Janelle stopped herself before she began bad-mouthing her brother-in-law. She'd ignored calls and texts from him for the past two days because she wanted to calm down before talking to him first. "It's going to take some time for everyone to deal with all of this."

"I know. But I still can't believe Dad cheated and he has another daughter. I mean, I always wanted a little sister, but not like this. She's almost as old as I am," Peyton said.

"Yeah, she is." Janelle sighed.

"Do you think she's going to come and live with us? I asked Mom earlier, but she didn't really have an answer."

"Um, I doubt it." Janelle prayed her sister wouldn't have to be faced with that decision. It was bad enough that Garry's little affair resulted in the birth of a child, but to have her come live in their home . . . no way. That was not happening.

"She doesn't have anyone else other than Dad. You think he's going to move out?" Peyton asked her.

"That might be a little more realistic."

"You think they're going to get a divorce? Peyton gasped.

"Peyton, calm down. I really don't know what's going to happen with them. What I do know is that both your mom and dad love you very much and will always be there for you no matter what. I know it's a lot going on, P., but trust me, it's all gonna work itself out. It's gonna take a little patience and time," Janelle said. This was Peyton's junior year of high school, and she had a lot on her plate. "And you know I love you, and I'm here for you too."

"I know you are, Aunt Nelle. Mom is so sad, though. I wish there was something I could do to make her feel better."

"She's going to be okay. Trust me, your mom is the strongest woman I know."

"Yeah, that's true. She is strong." Peyton laughed lightly. "I've felt her strength on more than a few occasions."

Janelle could hear the smile in her niece's voice, and she was somewhat relieved. "Haven't we all?"

"Thanks, Aunt Nelle."

"No need to thank me. That's what best friends are for," Janelle told her.

"Come on, Aunt Nelle. Everyone knows Nivea is your best friend. Oh, and Mom."

"Nivea is my homegirl, and your mom is my sister, but you are my bestie. Don't even try it. Why else would you call me if I wasn't your bestie?"

"You're right. Okay, fine, we're besties." Peyton gave in, and they both laughed.

"Damn right. Now, it's late. Go to sleep, bestie. You've got school in the morning."

"Good night, Aunt Nelle," Peyton told her. "I love you."

"Love you too."

As soon as the call ended, Janelle instinctively dialed Sylvia's cell phone, then remembered it wasn't working. She tried calling the house number, but no one answered. She closed her eyes and said a quick prayer for her sister. She couldn't imagine what she was going through. Hell, she was just as shocked by Garry's recklessness as everyone else. Next to her father, he was the closest thing to a perfect man that she'd ever known. Garry and Sylvia's relationship was the standard she used when it came to dating. She knew their marriage wasn't perfect, but their love was real, and she had always strived to find a guy who treated her the same way her brother-in-law treated her sister. He was affectionate, attentive, funny, dependable, and a good father and provider. On top of all of that, he was fine. To think that he'd cheated was unimaginable, and had it not been for the presence of his newly discovered child, she would have never believed it.

Garry was a good man. Or was he? How good could he be if he'd not only cheated on Sylvia, but lied about it and kept a secret this big for this long? There was no way Sylvia could stay with him, could she? Was their marriage strong enough to handle this?

Ring.

Janelle looked down and saw her sister's home phone number flashing on the screen. She immediately answered. "Hey, Syl."

"You called me?" Sylvia replied.

"I was just calling to check on you. How are you?"

"Please tell me that's a rhetorical question." Sylvia sighed.

"Actually, it's not. I really need to know how you're doing." Janelle could hear the frustration in her voice.

"I'm great, fantastic, super," Sylvia said, her voice dripping with sarcasm.

"Syl, you're not any of those things."

"You're right. I'm not."

"Is there anything I can do?"

"Unless you can erase the past week of my life, then no. There's nothing anyone can do."

"Well, I can't do that, but I can always come over with a bottle of Patrón and a bag of limes," Janelle suggested. To her relief, Sylvia laughed.

"As tempting as that sounds, I have to pass. You know I gotta take Peyton in the morning, and I can't do that if I'm hung over."

"You don't have to be hung over. We can just take a couple of shots."

"Trust me, I would take more than a couple. I'd probably drink the whole damn bottle," Sylvia told her. "But I'll take a raincheck. And trust me, I'll be using it soon."

Janelle reached for the soft throw blanket on the back of the sofa and spread it across her legs. "Hey, I'm ready when you are, sis."

"Can I ask you a question?"

"Sure thing."

"Do you think Garry loves me?"

Janelle frowned and sat up. She thought about all the questions she'd pondered a few minutes earlier. She realized that out of everything she'd asked herself, the one thing she hadn't wondered or doubted was Garry's love for Sylvia. Somehow, she knew that was real. You could see it in the way he looked at her and hear it in his voice when he spoke to her or talked about her.

"Yes, Syl, I do. I honestly do."

"I thought I did too."

"You don't think he does?"

"I don't know what to think. Hell, I thought he'd never cheat on me, but I was wrong about that."

"I don't think what he did had anything to do with his not loving you, Syl. Don't get me wrong; it's fucked up. Like, really fucked up. But it had nothing to do with his lack of love for you. Despite this horrible situation, I still believe what you and Garry have is special. You two have worked together and made shit happen: the house, the cars, your daughter. He's been behind you in everything you've wanted to do. You've got what people are out here searching for every day.

"But this is a lot for you to accept and forgive. I can't tell you what to do. That's all on you. Just think long and hard and know I got you. And if you still love him, there's nothing wrong with that. You can be pissed at him and still love him. Shit, I wouldn't even be mad if you wanted to stay with him. I love you, and whatever you decide to do, I'm right there with you. You wanna fight for your family, I'm right there fighting along with you and supporting you. You wanna leave his ass? I'll help you pack his shit because I know you ain't leaving that house."

"Thanks, Nelle," Sylvia said.

"No judgment, sis. But I'll tell you this: what you have ain't easy to find. Trust me, I know."

"I know too," Sylvia said. "And I appreciate you saying that."

"I love you."

"I love you too. Thanks for checking on me, and thanks for having my back."

"Anytime."

Getting off the phone, Janelle was glad Sylvia sounded better at the end of the conversation than she had at the beginning. She felt somewhat accomplished having assisted her sister and her niece. Now, if she could only be as insightful when it came to her own life.

Sylvia

Sylvia's office was in total disarray. After talking to Peyton and further discussing it with Garry, she had fully agreed and accepted the fact that Jordan would come and stay in their home. The house had a total of five bedrooms, one of which Garry himself would be moving into. Whether this would be a temporary move was still uncertain, though she kept saying that it was temporary. What was certain was the fact that Sylvia was an emotional wreck. The past two days were a blur. She barely remembered the moving company coming in and taking the furniture from the only downstairs bedroom, which she had been using as an office space, and moving it into the room over the garage. Instead of her massive oak desk, which held her computer and twenty-four-inch monitor, her comfy leather chair, and her file cabinets, the room now held a full-size bed, dresser, and night stand. Garry and his daughter were scheduled to arrive in two days, after Miranda's funeral had been held and her and Jordan's house was secured.

"Syl!" Lynne called her name.

"In here," Sylvia answered, smoothing out the comforter that she'd just placed on the bed.

"This is nice," Lynne said, walking into the room, which Sylvia had decorated in yellow and white décor. "It's very calm and inviting."

"Thanks. I don't know whether I should leave the TV in here or not," Sylvia said, pointing to the flat screen, which was still mounted on the wall.

"Do you have one upstairs already?" Lynne asked her.

"Yeah, but it's not this big."

Sylvia reached down and picked up a stack of folders from the corner, and they went upstairs into the room that was now her new office. She went to place them down and felt a tug at her heart when she saw that the stack included bridal magazines.

"Wow, this is huge," Lynne told her.

"Yeah, it's pretty big." Sylvia shoved the magazines into the bottom of one of the file cabinets that she now used to stash away anything wedding or bridal related.

"Even with the office furniture in here, you have a lot of space left."

"I think I'm gonna get a leather sofa and put it over there and get a small desk for Kenny, so he can have a workspace up here."

"Really?" Lynne smirked, "Don't you get enough of him at the office?"

"Okay, you're right. Maybe not." Sylvia laughed. "But you know we work here at the house a lot, especially when we have larger projects, which, by the way, we have going on right now. I feel bad that he's been doing all of the work. I haven't been much of a business partner the past few days. I can't focus on anything. Hell, I don't even remember us coming up here. I think I'm going crazy."

"You're not going crazy. And I know Kenny ain't saying nothing. We all know how much he loves being in charge with his controlling self. Not to mention there have been plenty of times when you have taken up the slack when he's had stuff going on. Remember when he almost had a nervous breakdown when he went through that breakup? Oh, and when his mom was sick."

Kenny rarely missed work, but those were two instances when he did take some much-needed time off and she handled everything. The breakup from his long-time girlfriend, Micah, had devastated Kenny, especially since soon after, he found out that she was pregnant by another man. A year later, Kenny had taken a short leave of absence to take care of his mother, who was diagnosed with cancer.

"So, when is she supposed to get here? What's her name again?"

"Jordan, and she is moving in Friday. The funeral is Wednesday, and they are tying up loose ends on Thursday."

"Have you talked to her?"

"Nope, not yet," Sylvia said. "I wouldn't even know what to say over the phone."

"Maybe you all should meet first before she moves in," Lynne suggested.

"Meet where? Golden Corral for breakfast?"

"Breakfast might be a good start. Just so the first time you lay eyes on each other isn't when she's moving into your house. Maybe it will break some of the tension that you know is about to be in here."

"Maybe. I don't know," Sylvia said.

"You're a better one than me, Syl, that's for sure. I don't know if I could let her move in. Garry and his kid would have to find somewhere else to go." Lynne sat in Sylvia's office chair and propped her legs up on the desk.

"I told you I'm crazy." Sylvia shrugged. "But Peyton was right. We're her family, like it or not. I don't know why, but when she said it, something in my spirit let me know that she was right. Kicking Garry out would have been real easy for me to do, but I don't know if that would have been the right thing to do. Even when I mentioned us separating, I knew it didn't feel right."

"Well, you vowed for better or for worse. I think this constitutes worse."

"It damn sure does," Sylvia told her. There was a knock at the front door, and then the doorbell rang several times. "Who the hell is that?"

They ran downstairs, and Sylvia opened the front door.
"About time. How long were you gonna let me stand
out here in the cold?"

Sylvia opened the door and let Aunt Connie in, carrying a suitcase in one hand and a crochet bag in the other.
With everything else going on, she had forgotten all
about agreeing to let her stay with them while the work
was being done at the senior citizens complex where
she lived. Sylvia began to do the math in her head. She
counted the number of bedrooms in their home, and the
number of people who would now be living there. Five
bedrooms for five people would probably be perfect math
if one of the bedrooms wasn't being used as her office.
Sylvia knew that she would have to continue sharing a
bedroom with Garry.

"For better or for worse," Lynne said, giving Sylvia a
hug of encouragement.

Sylvia took her best friend's advice and suggested to
Garry that they all meet for breakfast the day before
Jordan moved into the house. She, Peyton, and Aunt
Connie piled into her SUV and met Garry and Jordan
at an IHOP halfway between their home and Drakeville.
No one besides Aunt Connie really talked the entire
way there, and even she became quiet when they pulled
into the parking lot beside Garry. Seated beside him,
she could make out the shadow of a person who had to
be Jordan. He waved as he got out of his car, but the
shadowy figure remained inside.

"Hey, Daddy," Peyton said when her father opened the
rear door where she was sitting.

"Hey, sunshine." He kissed her on the forehead. Garry
then opened the door for Aunt Connie. "Hey, Aunt Connie.
I'm so glad to see you."

"Garry, nice to see you too. You know I got some choice words for you about this whole situation, but I'll save them for when you and I are alone," she said, giving him a hug and a kiss.

"Yes, ma'am. We'll have to sit down and have a talk." Garry nodded.

"Oh, trust me, we will be having several conversations, young man," Aunt Connie told him.

Garry looked over to Sylvia for help, but she offered none. He headed in her direction, and knowing he was going to try to open her door, she grabbed the handle and did it herself. She hopped out before he even made it to her side of the car.

"Good morning, Syl," he said.

"Good morning," Sylvia responded, walking past him and standing beside her aunt. It was freezing, and Sylvia was ready to get all of them out of the cold.

"Is that her in the car, Daddy?" Peyton asked.

"Yeah, sunshine." He nodded. "That's her. She's scared and sad. I told her she can take her time getting out."

"Should I go talk to her?" Peyton asked, looking at her mother for approval.

Sylvia admired her daughter's willingness to care for the girl, even under the uncomfortable circumstances. Peyton had a good heart, and it let Sylvia know that she had done a good job raising her. It was apparent that her loyalty in this ordeal was to her mother. Sylvia gave her a nod.

"If you want to," Garry encouraged their daughter.

"We're gonna go ahead inside and get a table," Sylvia said, taking Aunt Connie by the arm and leading her inside. "Come on, Aunt Connie."

They entered the restaurant, and the waitress seated them.

"You're a good woman, Sylvia. Your mama would be proud. You know that, right?" Aunt Connie told her with a nod of approval. Reaching across the table, she gave her hand a firm squeeze.

Sylvia looked over at her aunt, who looked so much like her mother that it was scary. "Yes, ma'am. I like to hope and think she would be. I wish she was here now more than ever, so I could talk to her."

"I miss her too, and even though she ain't here, I am. And I love you. I'ma say to you the same thing I know my sister would probably say."

"What's that?" Sylvia sighed.

"I know taking in Garry's child is not an easy thing to do, and although I want it to be smooth sailing for this family, it probably won't be."

"Aunt Connie, I'm not foolish enough to think we're gonna be the Brady Bunch." Sylvia shrugged, thinking that her mother probably would've said something a little more positive than what her aunt said.

"I just want you to know that I'm praying for you. And I'm here to help in whatever way I can. Now, you sure you're ready for this? Because if you are, I got your back. And if you aren't sure, then I got your back on that too. But this is a child's life that you're about to be dealing with—a child who just lost her mother, and you of all people know what that loss feels like. You've mourned the loss of yours."

Sylvia closed her eyes and let her aunt's words settle in her mind. She knew that although this decision was not an easy one to make—it may even be one she would regret when it was all over—but she did what her heart was telling her to do. There was no way she could see a young woman, whether it was Garry's daughter or not, go through the loss of her mother alone.

"I know I'm doing the right thing, and thank you, Aunt Connie." Sylvia reached over and grabbed her aunt's hand. As much as the woman got on her nerves, she was still her aunt, and she meant well.

Moments later, Garry and Peyton arrived at the table, followed by a beautiful young woman, looking very much like her husband.

"Mom, this is Jordan." Peyton did the introductions. "And this is Aunt Connie."

The girl looked at Sylvia briefly, then looked down at the table.

"Nice to meet you," Sylvia told her, hoping no one heard the nervousness in her voice. Her heart was racing, and she felt jittery even though she hadn't had her usual cup of morning coffee yet.

"Well, good morning, Ms. Jordan." Aunt Connie stood up and moved over, allowing Jordan to take the seat beside her. "I know you're glad to be able to eat something other than that hospital food, huh?"

Jordan gave Aunt Connie a puzzled look, then sat down and said, "Um, yes ma'am, I am."

"Then let's order you some pancakes! Where's that waitress? She ain't even brought us no hot coffee, but I bet she's gon' be looking for a tip when we leave."

There was no time for awkwardness or tension because Aunt Connie took over and dominated the entire breakfast conversation, as usual, talking about everything from the news to what Jordan's favorite foods were. And Sylvia was glad. She and Garry remained silent most of the meal and allowed Aunt Connie to serve as moderator between the family. By the time they finished eating, Sylvia felt a little more at ease about Jordan moving in.

Janelle

"She wants to go where?" Janelle asked.

"To a strip club called Mango's," Nivea answered.

"Wait, did you say strip club? Why the hell would Natalie wanna go to a strip club? Is it a male strip club?"

"No, it's a female one."

"Is she batting for the other team now?"

"Not that I know of. She wants us to meet her there at like eleven tonight. Do you wanna go? Where are you?"

Janelle looked at the time. It was after seven, and she was still running errands. "I'm at the pharmacy picking up my aunt's prescription, and I have to run to the store. I still don't understand why we are going."

"Me neither, but she is really hype."

"Wait, is she one of the strippers?" Janelle couldn't picture Natalie swinging on someone's pole. Maybe filing books away in someone's library, but a stripper, never.

"Hell no, she's not a stripper. She barely wears short sleeves in the summertime. You know she ain't taking her clothes off. I don't care who's making it rain."

"Oh, well, I guess we can go see what the hype is all about. I will call you when I get home."

Janelle pulled into the parking lot of the pharmacy and walked straight to the back to pick up her aunt's medicine. She was pleasantly surprised that instead of the regular pharmacist, there was a nice-looking black man behind the counter. The name on his tag read: ROD CRAWFORD.

"Picking up or dropping off?"

"Picking up for Connie Turner."

Janelle noticed his dimpled smile and dark, seductive eyes. Instinctively, her eyes scoped out his left hand for a ring, and she was happy when there wasn't one there. Not that it meant anything. She knew plenty of married men who didn't wear wedding bands.

"Here it is," he said, holding up the small plastic bag with three pill bottles. "Will there be anything else?"

"I need to get these too." Janelle handed him the small arm basket she carried with the rest of her items. The pharmacist took out the bottle of Centrum vitamins, the twelve pack of Ensure, and a pair of support pantyhose out of the basket then looked at her strangely. She was wondering why he paused until she remembered the box of magnums she had tossed in.

He smiled as he rang them up. "Will this be all, Mrs. Turner?"

"Yes, that will be it. And I'm not Mrs. Turner. She's my aunt." Janelle acted as if she wasn't embarrassed at all.

"Okay, then that will be forty-seven dollars and sixty-nine cents."

Janelle reached into her purse and handed him her check card.

"I'm gonna need to see some ID. Ms. Lee, is it?"

Janelle gave him her license, signed the receipt, and completed her transaction. "Thank you."

"Enjoy your night."

She laughed all the way to her car. She was still laughing about the incident hours later as she and Nivea walked through the doors of Mango's.

"At least he knows you have safe sex." Nivea snickered.

"I know it must've looked so random: all of those senior citizen goods, and then a box of magnums."

"Old people need love too!" Nivea giggled.

"Nivea, Nelle, over here," Natalie called.

They went over to the bar where she was sitting along with two other women. The club was crowded with male and female patrons. There were several strippers giving lap dances in the corner and scantily clad waitresses serving drinks. Rihanna's "Pour It Up" blasted from the speakers.

"I can *not* believe we are in a damn strip club." Janelle shook her head.

"Why not? It's so much fun. The music is live, and the drinks are banging!" Natalie told them. "And look around. This is where all the fellas are."

Janelle looked over to the group of men where Natalie was pointing. They all looked as if they were straight out of a rap video. "Uh, I don't know if I wanna date a man I met in a strip club. That don't seem right."

"Why not? It's some ballers in here, girl. The other night I met a guy who owns a Lexus dealership! And the week before that—"

"Oh my God, Natalie, how many times have you been here? Let me find out you're a regular at the strip club now." Nivea gasped. "Is that why you can't hang out with us?"

"You've been dissing us for the strip club? That is just wrong!" Janelle shook her head.

"Shut up," Natalie said and ordered a round of drinks.

It didn't take long for Janelle to sit back and enjoy herself. Natalie was right. The music was hype, and the drinks were amazing. They were having a great time when she looked up and saw a familiar face coming through the door.

"Oh my God," she hissed into Nivea's ear. "That's *him*!"

"Who?" Nivea looked over in the same direction as Janelle.

"Don't look. I don't believe it," Janelle said, trying be as discreet as possible so he wouldn't see her looking in his direction while talking about him.

"Who is it?" Nivea looked again.

Janelle was just about to explain who the guy was when suddenly her friend jumped up and ran over to the man Janelle was pointing out and hugged him.

"*Oh my God*! What are you doing here?" Nivea squealed in delight.

"Nivea, wow, I can't believe it's you!" he said with a wide grin on his face.

"This is crazy! I haven't seen you in forever."

The two walked over to the bar, and he noticed Janelle. Their eyes met, and they stared at one another. She tried to say something, but for some strange reason, no words came out of her mouth. She was rarely at a loss for words and figured it was happening now at the shock of not only seeing him in a strip club, but also the fact that Nivea knew him.

"Ms. Lee, right?" He smiled at her.

Janelle was glad that he spoke first, giving her a few more moments to get herself together. She sat up a little higher in her chair, making sure her body was situated perfectly, and quickly looked him up and down.

"How do you know each other?" Nivea asked.

"This is the pharmacist I was telling you about from earlier," Janelle told her.

"Oh, wow, that is hilarious. Sherrod, I didn't know you lived here."

"I just moved here a few weeks ago," he told them. "I'm still learning my way around town."

"Well, looks like you had no problem finding the strip club," Janelle said and gave him a slight smirk.

"That's true," Natalie agreed and nodded.

"One of my frat brothers is having a bachelor party. I normally wouldn't be in here. Well, I mean . . ."

"Rod!" a guy called across the club.

Rod waved over at the rowdy bunch. They were tossing dollars at the woman dancing in front of them. The group of about ten men were so loud and rambunctious that Janelle couldn't tell which one was the groom to be. It seemed as if all of them were intent on enjoying a last night of freedom.

"Well, we've gotta exchange numbers before you leave," Nivea told him.

"No doubt," he said, hugging her again. "Nice seeing you again, Ms. Lee."

"Same here," Janelle told him. "Don't make it rain too hard."

"Never that." He laughed and winked at her, causing her to raise an eyebrow at him.

Wait, is he flirting? She wondered as she watched him turn and walk away.

"How do you know him?" Janelle asked when they took their seats at the bar.

"We went to middle and high school together. He lived in our neighborhood," Nivea told her.

"Oh, okay." Janelle shrugged.

They went back to partying with Natalie and her friends. By the time they finished one drink, the bartender had placed another one in front of them, compliments of some dude in the club. One guy even sent one of the dancers over to give Nivea a lap dance, which she respectfully declined.

Janelle was having such a great time that she didn't realize she had several missed text messages until she took her phone out to check the time. Jarvis texted her twice, Titus three times, and her phone was now ringing with his number flashing on the screen.

"Hello," Janelle answered, covering one ear so that she could hear him over the loud music.

"Where the hell are you at?"

"Why?" Janelle asked.

"Because I wanna know."

"Nosey," she said, sucking her teeth as if she were frustrated by the call, which she wasn't.

"Where are you?"

"Mangos." She giggled, thinking of what his reaction would probably be.

"The strip club? What the hell are you doing there?" Titus laughed. "You into lap dances now?"

"As a matter of fact, I just had one," she lied. Janelle glanced up and saw Sherrod looking at her, smiling. She smiled back. "Look, I gotta go. It's loud in here."

She hung the phone up without hearing what Titus said. Nivea was up dancing with some guy, and Natalie danced with a girl. It was getting crazy. The later it got, the more people came into the club. It was nearly two a.m., and people were just arriving.

Her phone rang again, and she saw she had gotten another text from Titus. She was shocked when she read the words: come outside.

"I'll be right back," Janelle told Nivea.

"Where are you going?" Her friend frowned.

"I'll be back in a minute."

She grabbed her coat and slipped it on, heading out the door into the parking lot, where Titus flashed his lights at her. She walked over to his pickup truck, and he rolled down the window.

"What are you doing here?" she demanded to know.

"I came to check on you and make sure you were okay," he said. "This place can get real crazy."

"How do you know?"

"I've been here a couple of times." He shrugged.

"I bet." She laughed at him.

"Get in the truck."

Janelle looked around the parking lot. There was no one outside except the huge security guards posted in front of the club. The last thing she needed was one of her friends coming out and seeing her talking to him.

"No, I'm fine," she told him, shivering.

"It's cold as shit. Get into the truck. It's warm," he coaxed.

"No, I'm not gonna be out here that long."

"Get in and stop tripping."

Janelle relented and climbed into the truck beside him. They laughed and joked for almost thirty minutes before she told him she had to go.

"Why?" he asked.

"Because I've been out here long enough and my friends are inside," she said matter-of-factly.

"So it's like that? You don't wanna stay out here with me? I'm your friend," he leaned closer to Janelle and whispered in her ear. She felt his hands on hers, enjoying the warmth they provided. "Aren't I?"

"Yes, you're my friend." Janelle reached over and hugged him. She released from his grasp, opened the door, and got out. She waved at him and walked back toward the club. Just as she got to the front, she looked up and saw Sherrod Crawford staring at her.

Sylvia

Between Jordan, Aunt Connie, Garry, Peyton, and work, Sylvia's life was total chaos. She knew having Jordan move in was going to take some getting used to, but Sylvia did not know that meant having to deal with Gypsy, Jordan's one-year-old Pomeranian. The dog constantly barked, and although Jordan and Garry said she was trained, the puddles of pee and poop that Sylvia found all over her home showed otherwise. She wasn't necessarily a neat freak, but she took pride in keeping a clean house. Her newly acquired teen did not seem to have that same attitude, mainly because she had so much stuff that there didn't seem to be enough room to store it all. To say that Jordan was spoiled was an understatement. Clothes, shoes, purses, electronics, and then to top it all off, there was now a silver BMW in their garage that belonged to Jordan.

"She's not even old enough to drive," Sylvia said to Garry when she and Peyton came home a few days after Jordan arrived to find the car parked there.

"I know, and she doesn't drive it. It was her mother's old car, and she gave it to her when she got a new one," Garry told her. "I didn't see any harm in letting her keep it."

"You told Peyton she couldn't get a car until after she graduated from high school, and even then only if she had a three point seven GPA and got a scholarship. I've seen Jordan's grades, and they are nowhere near a two point five, Garry."

"I didn't give her the car, Syl. Her mother did. I had nothing to do with that," Garry responded as if it was no big deal.

"And the dog? How many times did Peyton ask for a dog and you flat out said no? It wasn't even up for discussion," Sylvia pointed out.

"Again, not my decision, Syl. I didn't give Jordan that dog." Garry shook his head.

"It seems to me that when it comes to Jordan, you really don't have a say so in any decisions that are made."

"What is that supposed to mean?" Garry said, putting the throw pillows onto the sofa of the sitting area in their bedroom. It was where he slept nightly. Although they still shared the master bedroom, there was no way she was going to allow him back into their bed any time soon. Garry had enough sense not to even ask. When their home was first built, he didn't understand why Sylvia was so bent on having the small den area in their room, along with the fireplace. She knew that he was grateful for it now. It was now his "room."

"Jordan didn't want to go to the academy with Peyton, so you allowed her to enroll in public school. Jordan doesn't want what we have for dinner, so you let her eat junk food in her room. What Jordan wants is what Jordan gets. And if you think for one moment Peyton doesn't see that, you'd better think again."

"Sylvia, it's not like that at all. I'm just trying to make her feel as comfortable as possible. She is going through a lot right now. Jordan just lost her mother. You of all people should realize how she feels. When your mother died—"

"Don't you dare! Don't you dare compare my mother's death and how I dealt with it to this situation! One has nothing to do with the other."

"I'm not saying that at all. I am just asking that you be a little more empathetic because it's not easy for her."

"For her? It's not easy for *me* or *Peyton*. Or have you forgotten that our lives have been disrupted too? Do you even care about how we feel or what we're dealing with? Oh, wait. It's only about Jordan now."

"It's not all about Jordan! It's about us as a family. We agreed that we would work through this situation *together,* and damn it, that's what I'm trying to do. What more do you want from me, Sylvia? Do you want me to leave? Would that make it easier? Right now, in this moment, it's *not* about anyone else but you. So tell me: what do you want?"

Sylvia stared at him, furious that he had put their family in this situation. Her life was one big ball of confusion, and there was so much going on that she sometimes didn't know if she was coming or going. She needed some space to think and some air to breathe. She wanted to run away and never come back.

No, what she wanted was her life back—the one she had two weeks ago when she was married to the man of her dreams, planning their vow renewal, and looked forward to what their future held. Now, within the blink of an eye and a forty-five second phone call in the middle of the night, it was gone, and she didn't know how to get her dream life back. Maybe that was all it was: a dream, a façade, a fictitious realm that didn't exist because she truly didn't know the man she'd married. So really, how could he be the man she thought he was? The man she married would never cheat on her, betray her, or break her heart the way that it had been broken.

"Yes." Sylvia looked into his eyes and told him, "Yes, I want you to leave."

"What?" Garry's eyes widened, and she could see the hurt in them.

"Leave. And take your daughter with you."

"Sylvia, please don't do this. In all the years we've been together, I made one mistake. *One.* I have been a good husband, a good friend, and a good father, but I made one mistake. You want to throw all of this away over one mistake?"

"If you were truly my friend, Garry, you would have come to me when you first made the mistake, and I would have forgiven you. But you didn't. Instead, you chose to lie to me for sixteen years. You lied to your wife and your daughter for over a decade and a half. Think about it. Does that truly make you a good husband or a good father?"

Sylvia didn't bother wiping the tears from her face as she turned to walk out of the bedroom. Before leaving, she looked back at Garry, who was still staring at her. She was surprised to see that he was also crying, and for a second, she felt satisfied that in that moment, he felt the pain that she was feeling.

Later that morning, after Garry had left for work and both girls were gone to school, Sylvia sat at the kitchen table across from Aunt Connie, drinking a cup of coffee.

"Aunt Connie, I know you hate walking up and down the stairs, so I'm gonna move you into the bedroom down here soon," she told her aunt.

Aunt Connie looked up from the Sudoku puzzle book she was writing in and said, "Child, I'm fine. The only time I go up there is when it's time to go to bed anyway. Besides, it would be too much work taking all that stuff Jordan has crammed into that room up them steps."

"Jordan won't be in that room much longer. She and Garry are moving out."

"Moving out? Why?"

"I told him I want him to leave. I can't deal with this. I thought I could, but it's just too much."

"Deal with what?"

Sylvia looked at her aunt like she was crazy. "You're trying to be funny."

"No, I'm not."

"Deal with all this." Sylvia tossed her arms into the air in exaggeration. "Garry, Jordan, his affair . . ."

As if she knew her name was going to be called next, Gyspy came running into the kitchen and hid under the table.

"This damn dog! This is exactly what I'm talking about. Jordan promised that the dog would be in the crate while she was at school. Now it's running around the house, pissing and crapping wherever she wants to. And who's gonna be the one to clean it up? Not Princess Jordan. Nooooo, that will be me!"

"Sylvia, calm down. I told Jordan to leave Gypsy out of the crate. It's not fair for that dog to be locked up all day, especially while I'm here in the house. And for the past couple of days, I've been letting her out to handle her business, so you really shouldn't have had to clean anything up. Jordan and I walk the dog every day when she gets home from school."

"You and Jordan?"

"Yes, *me* and Jordan. Well, Jordan and I. *We* do."

"Aunt Connie, I have never seen you and Jordan out walking the dog."

"That's because you're gone to pick up Peyton and running errands. Jordan gets home from school around that time. I make her some food, she eats, and we talk. After that, we take the dog out."

Sylvia frowned. "So, you feed Jordan dinner when she gets home from school?"

"Yeah, why wouldn't I? Dinner is already ready. You know that. And the child is starving when she gets here. She eats lunch at eleven in the morning. Y'all don't get back to the house until almost six o'clock and don't eat until seven. That's too long for that girl to wait."

"I didn't know," Sylvia said, surprised by what her aunt had revealed about Jordan's afternoon schedule.

"Well, now you know. So the dog problem is fixed. What else is it that you can't handle?"

"The fact that Garry caters to Jordan's every need. She gets everything she wants, but when it comes to Peyton, he is like an armed guard at a women's maximum security prison. Everything is: *'No, Peyton. That's not for you, Peyton. You're not ready, Peyton.'* It's not fair at all. Peyton is an honor student, a star athlete, and she's never been in trouble. When I went to register Jordan for school, you should've seen this girl's folder. She has been to detention more times this past year than they can even count, her grades are barely passing, and yet they reward her with a *car*?"

"I admit, Jordan does seem a bit spoiled, but I think she is just like most typical teenagers, and she gets away with what she can. She told me she always had to go to detention because she went to school late every day. Her mother managed a bar and didn't come home until almost four in the morning most nights, and Jordan would make her tea, and they would talk until they both fell asleep. I know you think it seems that she's had a good life, which she has, but so has Peyton in her own way. They are sisters, but you can't compare the two. That's like comparing you to Janelle. You got all the good grades, but Janelle was the party girl with all the cool friends."

"Garry thinks that this is just one simple 'mistake' as he calls it, and that it's fixable. It's more than that. It's a lie. I thought Garry and I had the kind of marriage that would not accept a lie. He's been lying to me for all these years. What else has he been lying about? Does he have a set of twin sons that are gonna come popping up on my doorstep any day now? I don't know if I can trust him again. How can I stay married to a man that I don't trust? That's what love is all about."

"You're right about that. But it's also about loving someone unconditionally."

"I do love Garry unconditionally."

"You can't say you love someone unconditionally until you've actually gone through some conditions. You always said that your entire marriage has been perfect. Well, now this is your storm. Are you gonna hunker down and weather it together or run away from it?"

Sylvia listened to the words of wisdom that her aunt was saying. She didn't know what to do. Never in a million years would she have ever believed that Garry would betray her like this.

"I don't even know how to start fixing this." Sylvia threw her hands up in frustration. Her aunt was making it seem like she was being unreasonable, which she knew she wasn't. Most women in Sylvia's situation wouldn't even be having this conversation because they wouldn't have done what she'd done. Instead, they'd be talking to a divorce attorney, or better yet, a shrink. But here she was, sitting across the table from the closest thing she had to a mother, so she listened to what Aunt Connie had to say and prayed it was going to not only makes sense, but be enlightening.

"You start by praying and asking God to heal your heart. That's the most important thing. Your marriage can't be healed if your heart isn't right. And even if you and Garry go your separate ways, you still need to heal. A wise man by the name of Al once asked me 'Connie, how can you mend a broken heart? How can you stop the rain from falling down? Tell me, how can you stop the sun from shining? What makes the world go 'round?' and I told him,

'Al, love and happiness, something that can make you do wrong, make you do right . . ."

"Aunt Connie, please stop. Those are all lyrics to Al Green songs. You are crazy. As a matter of fact, have you had your medicine today?" Sylvia stood up and walked over to the fridge, reaching on up top and passing her aunt the small basket that held her bottles of daily pills.

No luck on the enlightenment, she thought to herself.

"I don't need no pills." Aunt Connie took the basket from her and set it on the table. "What I need is for you to really think and pray and know that Garry is a good man, even though what he did was wrong. Hiding and lying only makes a bad situation worse. He knows that. But pray and seek godly counseling in this before you walk away from something that you say you can't handle. You're right; you can't handle it on your own. But with God on your side, you can go all the way. If the two of y'all want it, I lay my money on it. Starting today, you're going all the way!"

Sylvia reached into the basket and quickly opened the bottles of pills, pouring them into her aunt's hands. She smiled as she watched her mother's sister toss them into her mouth and finish her cup of coffee. She knew that her aunt was truly crazy, certifiably so, but she also knew that she was one of the wisest, strongest, and smartest women that she had ever known, and Sylvia was elated to have her in their house. After all, even with her plagiarized song lyrics, what Aunt Connie said really did make sense.

Janelle

Janelle was lonely. Not only had she not heard from Jarvis, but it had been days since she had spoken with Titus, although they had texted one another a few times. She missed speaking with him. She missed the intimate conversations and the laughter, the feeling of contentment when they shared their days with one another.

It had been a long week, and it was almost seven o'clock before she finally left work. She called Nivea, who didn't answer the phone. She spoke briefly to Sylvia, who was still dealing with the reality of Garry and his daughter. She was worried about her sister, but she knew after their last conversation that if she pressed, Sylvia would shut her out.

Thinking she would be spending her Friday night home alone, she decided to order some Chinese food and catch up on reality TV. Just as she pulled into the parking lot of the takeout restaurant, her phone rang. She looked down at the caller ID and smiled.

"Well, hello."

"Hey, you," Jarvis greeted her. "What are you doing?"

"About to stop and grab some food. What are you doing?"

"Trying to see you. I know it's last minute, but if you're up for dinner and a movie, I'd love to see you. Can you meet me at Kirby's in an hour?"

Dinner at Kirby's, one of her favorite steak houses, with Jarvis trumped her previous plans with beef and broccoli and the Housewives of Atlanta. Janelle made it home in record time, took a quick shower, changed, and was walking through the door of the restaurant within fifty-five minutes of talking to Jarvis.

"You look great." He smiled and stood up when she arrived at the table where he was already seated. "Then again, you always do."

"I can say the same thing about you, sir." Janelle put her arms around his neck, and he hugged her tight. She closed her eyes as she inhaled the scent of his cologne. When he released her, she took notice of the jeans he wore with a Polo sweater and boots. He was also wearing a pair of black-rimmed glasses that made him look even more sophisticated and attractive.

"So, what's been going on?" he asked after they placed their drink and appetizer orders.

They made small talk. She was tempted to ask him about Sade, but she didn't, reminding herself that Jarvis was not her man. Asking him about another female would be crossing a boundary that she may regret. Instead, she focused on enjoying the meal and the bottle of wine they shared.

After the check was paid, Jarvis looked at his watch and said, "We have about twenty minutes to get to the theater."

"I'm ready when you are."

They stood up, and he helped Janelle put her coat on.

She asked, "Do you want to drop one of the cars off at your place on the way?"

He smiled. "Does that mean we are going back to my place after the movie?"

"Do you want me to come back to your place?" she asked coyly.

"We don't even have to go to the movies if you don't want to." Jarvis raised an eyebrow at her.

"I want to," she said.

"Want to what? Go straight to my place?" he asked, and Janelle easily saw the lust in his eyes.

"No, go to the movies." She laughed. Janelle knew that she was going to go back to Jarvis's place the moment he called and asked her to dinner and a movie. She was horny, and Jarvis probably was too, which was most likely the reason for his last-minute request for the date. One thing Janelle knew was that men are creatures of habit, and Jarvis was no different. He never called at the last minute and asked her out on a date, so chances were, he'd had another chick cancel at the last minute and decided to hit her up to see if she was game. Heck, it had been almost a month since she'd had some good dick. *Why not?* But she was entitled to a movie first.

To her dismay and to Jarvis's delight, they hit traffic as soon as they left the restaurant and entered the highway toward his place. There was no way they would make the movie on time. When they finally pulled into his driveway, he got out of the car and walked to his front door.

"Where are you going?" she asked him.

"The movie started fifteen minutes ago. We missed it."

"How convenient?" Janelle said sarcastically as she followed him into his house. She removed her coat and sat on the sofa.

"You want something to drink?" Jarvis called from the kitchen.

"No, I'm good," she told him.

He came in and sat beside her. In a perfect world, Jarvis would have taken her into his arms, held her tight, and asked her about her week, or talked about what was going on in her life. Instead, he leaned over and kissed her for a little while, then stood up and reached for her. There was a noticeable bulge in the crotch of his pants.

"Come on. Let's go upstairs," he said.

Creature of habit, Janelle thought as she followed him upstairs.

A couple of hours later, as she was driving home, Janelle still felt as if something was missing. The sex with Jarvis was great, and she had no complaints. She was physically satisfied, but she still felt empty and wasn't ready to go home. It was after midnight. She didn't want to go to a bar or a club. She remembered her gym bag on the back seat and hoped a good workout would help release some of the frustration she was still feeling.

After changing clothes, she got in the zone, running on the treadmill to the sound of DMX until she was dripping with sweat. She walked over to grab a bottle of water out of the machine and noticed a guy waving at her from one of the weight benches. Just as she was about to ignore him, thinking he was some creep trying to holler, she recognized him and waved back, then walked over.

"Hey, Sherrod, right?"

"Hey, Janelle, right?" he said, shifting his body so that now he was facing her. "I tried speaking to you earlier, but you didn't see me. You were in your own little world."

"Yeah, that's what I do." She laughed. "I get in my zone, and nothing else matters."

"What are you listening to?" he asked.

Janelle realized her headphones were still playing and they were loud. "Oh, a little DMX."

"Hardcore workout music. I hear ya."

"And what you got playing?"

"John Legend."

"John Legend?" Janelle literally laughed out loud.

"I listen to mellow music when I lift." He shrugged. "I don't like to be too hype. Lifting is a process."

"A process, huh?" She giggled. "Sounds kinda soft to me, kinda like those biceps."

"What? You don't even believe that," Sherrod said, flexing his arms in front of her. "Feel that right there. Feel it."

Janelle rolled her eyes and then gently reached out and touched his arm. He was right. She didn't believe it when she'd said it. She had noticed his nice physique when she walked over to say hi to him. He wasn't muscular, but he had a nice, noticeable cut. He wore a white tank top, basketball shorts, and the same Nike Air Maxx that she had on.

"It's a'ight I guess," she told him.

"That's that power ball right there." Sherrod nodded.

"Whatever. So, you must be getting settled in and learning your way around town. You joined the gym and found the strip club."

"True. I am. So far, so good. How's your aunt? Still being safe, I hope."

Janelle tried not to blush. "The condoms were for her, I swear. Don't hate because my aunt gets her groove on."

"I'm not hating. I'm glad she's enjoying life at her age and being safe about it. That's the most important thing."

"I swear they were hers."

"And I don't—I mean, I do believe you."

They both laughed as she continued trying to explain to him about her loving but eccentric aunt, who had recently moved in with her sister and brother-in-law. She shared how her mother had passed away unexpectedly and how Aunt Connie had immediately stepped in and became their matriarch, although she was crazy at times and her mind drifted.

"Is it Alzheimer's?"

"No, it's not. She always drifted for as far back as I can remember. Even when I was little, she would just start saying speeches or singing songs out of the blue. She's just dramatic, like she is living her life out on stage. I know it sounds crazy, but we love her."

"She sounds lovable." Sherrod smiled, and he told her about his uncle who swore he was on tour with the Temptations and wrote "Tracks of My Tears" but never got credit for it. "He swore he came up with the dance moves and the whole nine yards."

"Was he on tour with them for real?"

"I can't say for sure, but I do know he played drums for James Brown. We have the pics to prove that."

"Where does he live now? We may need to hook him and Aunt Connie up." Janelle laughed.

"No way. Your aunt is already getting her groove on. I don't need my uncle involved in no love triangle. I don't care how safe she is."

Janelle laughed again. "There you go hating again."

"Am I interrupting?"

Janelle's heart dropped when she heard the voice behind her. She turned to see Titus standing in front of her.

"Titus," she said. "Um, no. This is Sherrod. He just moved here."

Sherrod stood up and shook hands with Titus. "Nice to meet you, man."

"Titus," Titus said.

"Well, I gotta be going," Sherrod said. "Nice seeing you again, Janelle. I am sure I will be seeing you around, especially when your aunt needs to feel safe."

"Whatever." Janelle smiled.

"Y'all seem cozy," Titus said when Sherrod walked away.

"He's cool." Janelle shrugged. "What are you doing here?"

"Looking for you. I thought I would surprise you, but I see I was the one who got surprised."

"How did you even know I was here? Stalking me again, I see."

"I saw your car while I was driving by. You know it's not really that safe for you to be coming to this gym in the middle of the night like this, right? You may run into some weirdo up in here."

"Like you?"

"More like him." Titus nodded toward the door where Sherrod was exiting. "I see y'all got the same taste in shoes."

"You are sounding quite jealous, you know that?"

"Me? Jealous? Never that." He playfully pulled the towel from around her neck. "You are looking good, Nelly."

Janelle nodded at him. "Well, it has been a while since you've seen me. I guess you've been really busy these days."

"Now who's sounding jealous?"

"Now, you know better than to even think that." Janelle reached over and took the towel from him and turned to walk away.

"You leaving already?"

"Yep. I've been here almost two hours."

"You weren't in such a hurry to leave when you were laughing it up wit' ol' boy."

Janelle stopped. "What? You're kidding, right? I haven't talked to you in almost two weeks, and you have the nerve to roll up in here talking sideways? Titus, please."

"Look, I'm sorry. That was wrong. And I know I've been kinda ghost, but I've been spending more time with Tarik. You know it's his senior year, and his team is doing great. Schools are recruiting him, and I'm trying to keep him focused."

Janelle knew there was some truth to what Titus was saying. His son had been highlighted on the local news for the past few weeks as one of the standout basketball players in the state. Seeing him made her wonder about her own child had she not made the decision that she did. Both children would be around the same age. Would her son or daughter have been an athlete like Titus had been, or would he or she have been a social butterfly like her? Janelle rarely allowed herself to think about the "what ifs" of that situation. When she did, she believed that her child would have been much like her niece, Peyton: the perfect balance of beauty, brains, and popularity.

"You know I miss you, right? How have you been?" Titus walked closer to her.

"I'm fine." She looked up at him and saw the love in his eyes and felt her heart flutter.

He touched the side of her face and rubbed her cheek. "You are fine, and beautiful, and amazing. I love you."

"I love you too," Janelle told him.

Titus leaned over and kissed her. In that moment, everything was instantly right in Janelle's world. She was no longer lonely, and the place in her chest that was empty when she first walked into the gym was now filled with everything she needed to feel.

Sylvia

"Can I spend the weekend at Meagan's?" Peyton walked into the den where Sylvia and Aunt Connie were folding laundry and watching a Lifetime movie. Gypsy, who had been lying on her pillow in the corner, jumped up and ran over to her.

"Don't you have track practice Saturday morning?" Sylvia asked.

"Yeah, but Meagan is on the team too. Her mom can take us," Peyton told her.

Peyton rarely asked to stay away from home overnight. That was probably due to the fact that it was something else her father didn't really approve of. Meagan and Peyton had been best friends and schoolmates for years, and Sylvia knew her family from church. Had it been anyone else, Sylvia would have instantly denied her daughter's request, but she didn't have a reason to say no, especially since Meagan had stayed over at their house several times.

"That sounds like fun. I used to love slumber parties when I was your age," Aunt Connie volunteered, then suggested, "Why don't you invite Jordan?"

Sylvia and Peyton both looked at their aunt like she was the crazy woman everyone believed she was. Gypsy kept jumping and playing at Peyton's feet. Peyton made it a point to ignore the dog at all times, often commenting that it wasn't hers to play with.

"I don't think so," Peyton said.

"Why not?" Aunt Connie asked. "She needs to make some new friends here."

"She has enough friends. Have you seen her Facebook page?" Peyton shook her head. "Move, *dog*!"

"Stop yelling at her. She just wants you to pick her up," Aunt Connie told her. Gypsy ran over to Aunt Connie, who picked her up and placed the small dog into her lap.

"I haven't seen her Facebook," Sylvia said. "What's on it?"

Peyton shrugged nonchalantly. "Nothing really. She just has a lot of friends, that's all. Besides, practice on Saturday is closed, and they don't allow anyone there. Can I please go?"

"Then you should invite Meagan and y'all can have a sleepover here instead." Aunt Connie passed Peyton the pile of neatly folded clothes. "Here, these are yours."

"Thank you," Peyton said. "Mom, can I?"

Sylvia looked at her daughter. "Yes, Peyton, but I need to talk with Meagan's mom and confirm all of this."

"I know you do, Mom." Peyton leaned over and kissed her mother's cheek. "I love you, Mom, and you too, Aunt Connie!"

She ran out of the room and Sylvia couldn't help but smile. Peyton deserved a break. She was dealing with this situation the same as everyone else. Sylvia was determined that even though this ordeal was disruptive and problematic for all of them, it wouldn't have an adverse effect on Peyton's life. She wanted her life to remain as normal as possible—ell, if that was even possible.

"Where is Jordan anyway?" she asked Aunt Connie, who always seemed to know more about Jordan than anyone else in the house other than Garry.

"She went to the library to work on a project. Garry dropped her off and is picking her up."

"Oh, what kind of project?" Sylvia asked.

"Why don't you ask her yourself?"

Sylvia had tried talking to Jordan, but unlike the way she seemed to be with Aunt Connie, the girl was distant and guarded. She was polite, but there was a wall up, and Sylvia wasn't sure that she even wanted it to come down, especially now that she had asked Garry to leave. There was tension in the home, and everyone was walking on eggshells, except Aunt Connie.

"She's not my problem," Sylvia said, wanting to point out that Jordan was Garry's daughter, not hers.

"She's not anyone's problem. She's a child. A child who just lost her mother and is now living with her father and a woman who acts like she doesn't like her."

"No, she acts like she doesn't want to be here," Sylvia said, instantly becoming defensive.

"Would you?" Aunt Connie asked. "Come on, Gypsy. Time for you to go outside."

Sylvia didn't answer her. She picked up the pile of clothes that belonged to Jordan and took them into her room. As usual, there was stuff everywhere. She didn't know where to put any of the items, so she laid them on the unmade bed. A pair of socks rolled off and onto the floor. Sylvia leaned over to pick them up when she spotted a colorful, cardboard box in the corner. It had stickers and drawings on it and the words *The Magical World of Jordan*. Curious as to what was inside, Sylvia peeked in it. She saw what looked like binders that someone had made into scrapbooks and photo albums.

She reached in and pulled out one binder. The pink foil cover read *The Beginning*, and inside was everything from Jordan's conception and first year of life: ultrasound photos, reminder cards for doctor's appointments, and a baby shower invitation announcing *It's a Girl!* There was even a page that contained a neatly folded Hostess cupcake wrapper, remnants of foil from Hershey's kisses, and the label from a chocolate Yoo-Hoo taped to it. *I crave anything chocolate, so I know she will be sweet!* was written on the bottom.

Sylvia turned the page, and her heart nearly stopped. There were pictures of a woman from each month of her pregnancy. She realized it was Jordan's mother, Miranda. On one hand, Sylvia wanted to shut the book tight and throw it back into the box, but she couldn't. She looked at the pictures of the woman and studied them. As much as Sylvia thought Jordan looked like Garry, she also looked a lot like her mother. They had the same high cheekbones and thick eyebrows. She was a beautiful woman who seemed to be enjoying every moment of her pregnancy.

Sylvia continued flipping through the pages, taking it all in. She came to the page that celebrated the day of Jordan's birth, the Fourth of July. According to the birth announcement, Jordan was born at 6:37 a.m., weighed eight pounds six ounces, and measured twenty inches long—much bigger than Peyton, who had weighed only six pounds two ounces. Garry had been adamant during Sylvia's entire pregnancy that she stuck to a healthy diet and stayed away from sugar. Clearly, he didn't make those same stipulations to Randy.

Sylvia turned the page, and sure enough, there was a picture of Garry holding a newborn Jordan, smiling with pride. Sylvia quickly tried to think back, but she knew Garry was always home for the Fourth of July holiday. He had never missed one. She wondered how in the world he could have been in two places at the same time. She looked closer at the picture and realized it was taken two days later when Randy and Jordan were released from the hospital.

Sylvia became engrossed in the photos and memories that Randy had so meticulously recorded of the first fourteen years of Jordan's entire life. From first steps and first words to each and every holiday, birthday, and school event, nothing was left out. The weird thing was that Garry was in most of the pictures. Her husband truly had been living what was a double life.

Sylvia kept going through each binder, one by one. When she completed one, she'd reach into the box and pull out another. She knew she was invading something private and intimate, but she couldn't stop herself. Just as she opened the third book, a white envelope fell out and into her lap. Sylvia picked it up and was shocked to see that it was addressed to her. She looked around to see if there was a hidden camera somewhere in the room because someone was pulling a prank on her. She didn't know what to do.

"What are you doing?"

Jordan's voice startled her, and Sylvia nearly jumped off the bed. She slipped the envelope into the back of the binder and closed it tight. "Hey, Jordan. How was your day?"

"Fine," Jordan said. "What are you doing in here?"

Sylvia looked at her, dressed in the fitted pair of jeans, crop top sweater, and combat boots, looking teenage-chic with her long hair piled into a bun on the top of her head, shiny lip gloss, and dangling earrings. It was a fashion look any girl her age strived for daily, and Jordan had it mastered. Garry's daughter definitely had style and a taste for fashion.

"I was, um, putting your clothes away . . . and then, the socks fell and rolled over by this box . . ." Sylvia hesitated. "And then I was picking them . . . um, I was picking them up and saw the box. . . ."

"So, you went in my memory box?" Jordan frowned.

Suddenly feeling bad, Sylvia quickly passed the binder she was holding out to Jordan. "I did, and I apologize."

Jordan took the book from her and stared. "You looked at my memory books?"

"Yes, they are beautiful, and so is—was . . . your mother."

Jordan seemed surprised by Sylvia's statement. "Thanks. She was."

"I can't believe she kept all of those memories of you. She loved you very much." Sylvia smiled.

Jordan nodded. "I was her miracle. I saved her life."

"How?"

"I don't know. It's just something she always said." Jordan shrugged and continued staring at the book she was now holding.

Sylvia reached over and touched Jordan's shoulder, and she slightly flinched. Not wanting to make her any more uncomfortable than she already was, Sylvia just said, "You're beautiful like she was."

"You think so?" Jordan's voice was barely above a whisper.

"Yes, I do," Sylvia told her as she turned to walk out of the room.

"Wait," Jordan called after her, and held the book out to Sylvia. "You can take it if you want. Just bring it back."

"Thank you, and I will," Sylvia assured her as she took the book into her hand. Jordan seemed pleased that Sylvia took it.

Sylvia went upstairs into her office and closed the door behind her. She sat down and called Lynne, telling her about finding the memory book and getting caught by Jordan. She also told her about the letter addressed to her from Miranda.

"What does it say?" Lynne asked.

"I don't know. I didn't open it." Sylvia made sure to lower her voice. Even though her door was closed, she didn't want to chance anyone hearing her conversation, especially Aunt Connie, who was normally hard of hearing yet seemed to have supersonic hearing when it came to conversations like the one she was having now.

"Why not?" Lynne sounded confused. "What are you waiting on?"

"Because I . . . it's . . . hell, I don't know," Sylvia stuttered as she stared at the colorful binder that was now sitting in the middle of her desk.

"It's yours. It's addressed to you. Open it and read it," Lynne told her.

There was a knock at the office door, startling Sylvia. She became nervous until the door opened and Kenny walked in.

"I gotta go. Kenny's here," Sylvia told her.

"Call me after you read the letter!" Lynne yelled through the phone just as Sylvia was hanging up.

"Who the hell was that?" he asked, looking at her strangely.

"It was Lynne," Sylvia said simply as if it was no big deal.

"Are you sure? Because you're acting like you sneaking on the phone talking to your side piece and ain't tryna get caught."

"You know I ain't got a side piece," Sylvia snapped.

"Fine, your side boo," he said, placing his leather laptop bag in one of the chairs.

"You're not funny." Sylvia gave him an aggravated look.

"I'm serious. You may have gone out and met a guy to get back at Garry, who I noticed is still here. I thought you kicked him out." Kenny seemed slightly amused, which annoyed her even more.

"I did. I told him he had thirty days," Sylvia said adamantly. She knew where Kenny was headed and wanted to stop him before he started.

"He ain't going nowhere." Kenny laughed loudly.

"Shhhhh! Stop being loud before someone hears you," Sylvia snapped.

"Oh, my bad," Kenny whispered and dabbed at the tears that had formed in his eyes.

Seeing his amusement frustrated Sylvia even more than she already was. "And like I told you, he ain't staying here!" she snapped. "This is just a temporary situation until he figures out a living situation for him and his other daughter."

"Nah, it's not. The way I see it, if you loved him enough to let him stay a month ago when all this came out, then there was something inside that gave you enough hope to see this thing through," he pointed out to her.

"Well, maybe it was temporary insanity. Whatever it was just isn't there anymore. It's gone. Or maybe I was still in shock and stupid enough to believe we could work it out." Sylvia shook her head.

"Or maybe you need to dig a little deeper and find whatever it was. Come on, Sylvia. I know you. You have loved Garry from the moment that dude said, 'Can I get a large fry and a strawberry shake?' that day he was standing in front of you in McDonald's line. And he loves you." Kenny laughed. "You ain't gotta front for me. I was there from day one."

"I can't believe you remember that." Sylvia half-laughed.

The day she met Garry, she'd told Kenny she met the man she was going to marry. At first, he didn't believe her, but soon, not only did he see that she and Garry were meant to be, but everyone else did too. There was something about him that instantly let her know that they were created for one another. She had never felt it with anyone else. It was love. But now she had learned that he had loved Randy, too, for the past sixteen years. That fact made her realize that as much as she loved, trusted, and believed that she was meant for Garry, maybe he wasn't meant for her. How can you keep a secret for a decade and a half from someone you love? Especially one as big as this?

"He's a liar and a cheater." Sylvia frowned.

"Like Aunt Connie told me a few minutes ago, the only perfect man to walk this earth was Jesus. That's why she doesn't mind me being a man whore. She loves me anyway." Kenny grinned.

"His mistress wrote me a letter." Sylvia opened the binder up and pulled the envelope out for Kenny to see.

"She did? Now, that's gangster. What does it say? Who gave it to you?" Kenny reached for the letter, but Sylvia snatched it back.

"No one gave it to me. I found it when it fell out of one of Jordan's baby books. I haven't read it yet." She sighed and stared at the envelope.

"Why not? You scared? I would be. I can't even front. A letter from your husband's dead mistress? Now, that's scary," Kenny stood back and folded his arms.

"I'm glad you find all of this amusing, Kenneth, because I don't." Sylvia sat back in the chair and stared at the letter.

"Open it. Read it," he told her.

"I don't want to. Why should I? I don't want to hear about how much she loves Garry and how they want to be a family." Sylvia sighed.

"Maybe that's not what she says."

"Right before you got here, I spent damn near an hour going through *The Magical World of Jordan*. Her mother captured every single moment of this girl's life. She was intense, graphic, detailed, and passionate about any and everything her daughter did. I can only imagine what that woman put in here. Oh, and she was beautiful. Look." She opened the binder up and passed it to him so he could see for himself.

"Daaaaamn," Kenny said as he flipped through the pictures of Miranda. Then, realizing how his response must've sounded to his best friend, he tried to clean it up. "I mean, she a'ight."

"Screw you." Sylvia glared at him.

"Oh, no. You won't be using me to get back at Garry. Now, read the damn letter," he told her.

"You read it." She picked up the letter and held it toward him.

Kenny didn't need to be told twice. He reached over and snatched the envelope, holding it up to the light. "I'll be damned. She really did write you a letter. I wonder how old it is. I wonder why she never mailed it."

"Just read it, please," Sylvia said under her breath.

"You sure?"

"Yeah, I'm sure."

Sylvia held her breath as Kenny carefully opened the envelope addressed to her in the fancy cursive writing. She closed her eyes and waited for him to reveal all that Miranda Meachum had to say.

Janelle

"I just have two more stops to make, sweetie. I sure appreciate you getting me out of the house to run my errands today."

"You know I don't mind, Aunt Connie," Janelle lied. She had been taking Aunt Connie all over the city since nine o'clock in the morning. It definitely was *not* how she had planned on spending her Saturday, but when her aunt called and asked her to come pick her up, she knew there was no way she could say no.

"Normally, Sylvia takes me to do this, but you know she got a lot on her plate right now. Have you talked to her?" Aunt Connie asked.

"Not about what's going on. I tried, but I get the feeling that I'm the last person she wants to talk about that situation with." Janelle sighed. The few times she'd reached out to Sylvia, her sister seemed irritated. Their normal hour-long conversations had turned into five-minute chats. When Peyton called to tell her about Jordan moving in, Janelle immediately called her sister to find out what was going on, but the only thing Sylvia told her was that it was just until Garry "figured it out."

"Because of you and Titus probably," Aunt Connie told her.

"What?" Janelle was shocked by her aunt's statement.

"You and Titus. It bothers her," Aunt Connie said.

"I don't know what you're talking about, Aunt Connie." Janelle decided the easiest way to respond was to act as if she were clueless.

"Girl, don't play dumb with me. You think I don't know that you're still seeing him and have been for years now?" Aunt Connie cut her eyes at her.

"I haven't been seeing him. Not like people think. He is my friend and he always will be. And why does it bother her? She shouldn't feel some way about me because we're still friends. She's still friends with Kenny, and they dated back in the day. They've been friends just as long as me and Titus. What's the difference?" Janelle tried to sound as innocent as she could.

"There is a big difference, and you know it."

"Aunt Connie, despite what you and everyone else may think, I am *not* sleeping with Titus," Janelle said, wondering how her aunt even knew about their continued friendship. She must've heard it from Sylvia.

"Well, Kenny and your sister never did either, *and* they were never in love with one another. You and Titus have done *both* of those. Now, you may not be having sex now, but you have had sex while he is married," Aunt Connie said matter-of-factly.

Janelle shook her head. Her aunt was right. For the most part, she and Titus were just friends, but there had been times when they gave in to temptation and met at a local hotel and satisfied one another like they both knew no one else could. He was her Kryptonite. He made her weak and vulnerable, even though she tried to resist. It had been months since they had made love, not since she started dating Jarvis. She had hoped that somehow, he would be a welcomed distraction.

"People don't understand. What Titus and I have, it's indescribable. What we feel for one another, the friendship we have, whatever it is, it's kismet. You don't get it. You met and married Uncle Mick right out of high school," Janelle told her.

"Honey, I met my soul mate years ago. He is the one man who knows me better than anyone, the one I connect with on all levels. The one who makes me feel like no one else ever can. He is the one I feel like I was created for, and the one the good Lord created for me. Too bad I was already married to your uncle, God rest his soul, when I met him. Just because someone is your soul mate doesn't mean that's the one you're destined for or the one you'll end up being with. Trust me, I know, and I struggle with that thought even today." Aunt Connie stared at her.

Janelle couldn't believe what her aunt had said. It was as if she knew exactly how she felt. "Aunt Connie, did you cheat on Uncle Mick?" she whispered.

"I did. And it's not something I'm proud of, but in my heart of hearts, I don't regret it in some ways. But, Janelle, just because something is meant to happen doesn't mean it's meant to be. You don't need to confuse the two." Aunt Connie touched her shoulder and gave it a slight squeeze.

Janelle could see the emotion in her eyes and knew that this conversation was one that had been a long time coming. "Aunt Connie, I'm not. I date other guys. You know that. But they don't make me feel anything near what I feel for Titus. After all these years, he's still the one for me," she explained.

"One of the worst feelings in the world is knowing you both love one another but you can't be together. But you ain't doing nothing but torturing yourself. I hope you ain't foolish enough to believe he's leaving his wife to be with you," Aunt Connie snapped.

"No, I don't. We've never even talked about that. We are just friends at this point." Janelle told her, "I don't expect anything from him. But even with the other guys I've dated, it doesn't feel the same."

"Well, maybe that's your problem and why you can't *feel* for anyone else. You don't need to because you're getting all 'feeled up' by Titus, and that's just wrong. Oh, wait. Pull over to the pharmacy. I need to run in there." Aunt Connie pointed out the window.

Janelle pulled into a parking spot close to the door.

"Aunt Connie, did Uncle Mick know about you and your soul mate?" Janelle asked.

"He did." She nodded.

"What did he say?"

"He was hurt, but he forgave me eventually. When he got angry at times, he would bring it up, and one time, he even said that the reason we never had a child was because God was punishing me for what I did." Aunt Connie's voice softened, and Janelle saw her eyes water.

"That was mean. I'm sorry." She shook her head.

"I had to explain to him that I serve a merciful God who forgave me the same way I forgave him for a whole lot of stuff he did. And I told him he was not gonna keep crucifying me over and over for the same sin, and if he kept it up, I was gonna cut him and leave him for dead where no one would ever find his ass."

Janelle burst out laughing at the thought of her aunt threatening her uncle with a knife. "Aunt Connie, you are crazy!"

"No! Well, maybe so. But he knew I was telling the truth, and I bet he never brought it up again and we lived happily ever after. You know, I once told your mama that when a man loves a woman, he can't keep his mind on nothing else. If she is bad, he can't see it. She can do no wrong; turn his back on his best friend if he put her down."

"Aunt Connie, you do know that's a Sam Cooke song, right?" Janelle pointed out.

"Shut up and listen to me. There is nothing like the love of a good man, that's for sure. That's why I keep telling Sylvia to fight for Garry. He's a good man, and she's a good woman, just like me and your uncle, and your mama and your daddy. We ain't perfect, but we were good people, and we fought to hold on. You need to find someone worth fighting for, and who will fight for you. That's what love is all about. It's not about feeling good all the time or matching your soul. The truth is our souls belong to the Lord, and while we worried about who our mates are on earth, we need to be doing what we need to do to get to heaven. Find that person who will be in the ring for you, Janelle. That's the one you wanna be with," Aunt Connie told her.

"Yes, ma'am." Janelle leaned over and hugged her aunt.

"Now come on, because I need to get some Epsom salt and some witch hazel. Oh, and some Pink Oil Moisturizer for my hair," she said as she opened the car door and stepped out.

Janelle followed her aunt into the store and grabbed a basket. Her eyes went to the back of the store where the pharmacy was located, and she searched for Sherrod but didn't see him. For some reason, she was slightly disappointed. She thought about their conversation at the gym the night before and how much she had enjoyed it.

"You ladies finding everything you need?"

She turned around to see him standing in the aisle, smiling.

"Yes, sir, we're fine. How are you?" Janelle asked.

"I'm great. Is this your aunt I've heard so much about?" He nodded toward Aunt Connie.

"Yes, this is Aunt Connie. Aunt Connie, this is Sherrod Crawford, the pharmacist." Janelle introduced them.

"Nice to meet you, ma'am." Sherrod extended his hand.

"Same here, young man. But please don't call me ma'am." Aunt Connie shook his hand. "Call me Connie. And where is your Epsom salt?"

"It's right over here." Sherrod led them to where she could find it. "You need anything else?"

"I think I have everything else." Aunt Connie looked in the basket to make sure.

"I can check you out back here," he told her. "Follow me, Ms. Connie. It is Ms., isn't it? Or is it Mrs.?"

"It's Ms., but I'm not available at the moment, in case you were wondering." Aunt Connie told him. "I'm currently *involved*."

They went to the register, and he rang the items up, making small talk with Aunt Connie about the meds she was taking.

"Wait, where are your condoms?" Aunt Connie asked.

Janelle gave him an 'I told you so' look and waited for him to respond.

"Uh, they are right over here," Sherrod told her, pointing to the rack. "Any particular brand?"

"Magnum, the ones in the black box," Aunt Connie replied.

Sherrod grabbed the small box and went to ring it up.

"No, get me the big box," Aunt Connie told him.

"Aunt Connie," Janelle whispered, "I just bought you a box less than a month ago. What in the world?"

"You can never be too safe. That's what I told Peyton when I gave them to her."

"Peyton? Why does Peyton need condoms?" Janelle was shocked at the thought of her niece having sex. She didn't even know she had a boyfriend. "Is she having sex? Does Sylvia know?"

"I don't know if she's having sex or not. I know she likes boys because I hear her talking on the phone. And if she likes boys, then I'm sure boys like her, and you know what happens when boys and girls start liking each other. Didn't you and I just have a talk about you feeling some kind of way about Titus?" Aunt Connie smirked.

Janelle glanced up to see if Sherrod was listening. Based on the look on his face, not only did he hear the conversation, but he was amused by it. Janelle could feel the heat rising in her cheeks. She had never been so grateful for her mocha complexion as she was at that moment.

"Just because she likes a boy doesn't mean they are having sex," Janelle leaned over and told her.

"Well, in case she decides to have sex with the boy she likes, she will be prepared," Aunt Connie said. Then she looked up and asked, "Don't you think teenagers need to be prepared? As a matter of fact, can you hand me another box for my niece here? I need for her to be prepared too."

"You're absolutely right," Sherrod said. "Do you need Magnums, or will Trojans suffice?"

"Umph, I hope she got more than a Trojan man in her life." Aunt Connie laughed as she took the money out of her wallet and passed it to Sherrod to pay for her items.

"I don't need any, thank you very much. And you can put that box back too. Peyton doesn't need them either, Aunt Connie. Sylvia and Garry would be pissed if they knew you were giving Peyton condoms."

"They would be even more pissed if she came up pregnant, or worse, had AIDS."

"She won't. Peyton is a good girl. And I will talk to her, I promise." Janelle knew her aunt meant well, but her methods were a little eccentric and extreme. She could only imagine Peyton's face when Aunt Connie gave her the box of Magnums, and she prayed her aunt hadn't mentioned anything about a "Trojan man" to her innocent niece.

"Okay, well, if you say so. Sherrod, are you married?" Aunt Connie asked.

Sherrod coughed and said, "No, I'm not."

"Do you have a girlfriend?" She continued.

"Not right now, I don't," he said.

"Well, I'm sure you have sex. Do you need any condoms? I already paid for them." She took the condoms out of the bag and handed them to him.

"No thanks, Ms. Connie. I'm good," he told her, looking surprised.

Janelle leaned over and whispered loudly, "I think he might be a Trojan man."

Sherrod's jaw fell open, and the look on his face was priceless. Janelle gathered her aunt and her bags and waved goodbye as they walked away.

"Now, he is cute, and he is single," Aunt Connie said when they got in the car. "You better get on that."

"Aunt Connie, you need to stop," Janelle said.

"Oh, let me run in the Dollar Store right quick while we are over here. Come on."

"You go ahead. I will wait here," Janelle said.

Her cell phone rang, and she answered it. "Hey, Nivea girl."

"Hey. I saw you called last night. I was 'sleep and missed everybody's call: you, Natalie, Sherrod."

Janelle felt a tinge of jealousy when Nivea mentioned Sherrod calling her. She almost asked why he was calling, but she stopped herself. She also didn't mention that she had just seen him at the pharmacy.

"I didn't want anything." Janelle sighed.

"What did you do last night?" Nivea asked.

"Went out with Jarvis and then hit the gym for a little while," Janelle told her.

"You had enough energy to go to the gym after a date with Jarvis? He musta been whack." Nivea laughed.

"Naw, he was okay. I just wasn't ready to go home yet." She sighed.

"Or was there some other reason you wanted to go to the gym? Go ahead and say it." Nivea exhaled loudly.

"Say what?" Janelle questioned her friend. She wondered if Nivea had spoken with Sherrod and he mentioned seeing her at the gym.

"That's where you meet up with Titus, isn't it? Your rendezvous spot. Was he there?"

"Yeah, he was," Janelle confessed.

"I knew it! I swear you are a mess. You know if Jarvis finds out you left him to go see another dude, that's it, right?" Nivea told her.

"First of all, Jarvis and I are just friends, so he can't say anything about me seeing anyone. He sees other people all the time. And I didn't go to the gym planning to see Titus at all. He stopped when he saw my car in the parking lot," she explained, not wanting her friend to think seeing Titus was planned, which it wasn't.

"If you say so. Well, I gotta go. I have a hair appointment. I'm meeting Sherrod later for drinks and appetizers and to catch up on old times, I guess," Nivea told her, again causing a twinge of jealousy for some reason.

She wanted to ask Nivea who invited who out, but her best friend had just pointed out that she spent the night before with two guys, one of whom happened to be married, so she decided it was none of her business. Besides, she wasn't even sure if she was interested in Sherrod, really. Sure, he was good looking and seemed to be nice, but so were a lot of guys, including Titus and Jarvis.

"Really?" Janelle said. "Well, you guys have fun."

"I am definitely gonna try. I'll call you tomorrow." Nivea sounded a little more excited than Janelle wanted her to sound.

"Okay, cool," she said dryly.

"And Janelle?" Nivea yelled just before Janelle ended the call.

"Yeah?"

"Stay outta the gym."

Janelle faked a laugh and hung up the phone. Suddenly, she had a slight headache, and she was ready to go home, get into bed, and sleep the rest of the weekend away.

Sylvia

"Why can't I go? I've been here almost a month. I miss my friends, and I want to hang out. Why are you making this so difficult for me?" Jordan yelled from downstairs. "Why can't I go?"

Sylvia walked closer to her office door so she could get a better listen to what was going on downstairs. Garry and Jordan had been arguing all morning because Jordan was homesick and begging to go back.

"Look, I said I would take you back for a visit, and I will when I get time."

"I don't need you to take me. I can go and come back tomorrow," Jordan said. "This is *not* my home. This is *your* home. I didn't want to be here; you made me come here. No one even wants me here! I am almost sixteen. I have a car, and I know Mom left me the townhouse and some insurance money. I could have stayed and taken care of myself," she cried.

"Jordan, you're being ridiculous. There was no way you were staying there alone."

"I didn't have to be alone. I could have stayed with Doc. He even said—"

"Stop it. There was no way in *hell* I was leaving you with him."

"Why not? He loved *me,* and he loved my mama!"

"No, Jordan."

"You let her go away for the weekend to spend time with her friends. Why can't I? I wanna go home."

Sylvia held her breath, waiting to see what Garry's response would be, especially about Peyton. She knew Garry wasn't too happy when he found out Peyton was spending the weekend with Meagan. She'd been waiting for him to say something to her about it, but he had sense enough not to.

Garry said, "Jordan, this is your home. And you can't go back there right now. You know how I feel about him. He's not your fa—"

"You don't have to remind me of that." Jordan jumped up and stormed off.

"Jordan, come back here! Don't you walk out of that door!" Garry shouted after her.

The door slammed so hard that Sylvia winced. She wondered who Doc was and what Jordan meant. A few moments later, she heard Garry climbing the stairs. She hurried back over to her desk and sat down. She hadn't really said anything to her husband after giving him his thirty-day notice nearly a week ago. She hadn't brought it up, and neither had he. She did see a real estate guide lying on the front seat of his car, but that didn't necessarily mean he was looking for a place to go.

Sylvia thought about the letter that Randy had written her. Both she and Kenny had been surprised by what the woman had to say, and in a way, Sylvia could relate. Suddenly, she heard a weird sound coming from their bedroom. Sylvia walked into the hallway and listened closer to what sounded like a muffled whimper, and she realized it was Garry. Her husband was crying. In all her years of knowing him, Sylvia had never seen her husband shed a tear, except when he witnessed Peyton's birth. One of the things she loved about Garry was that he was the strong, silent type. During the loss of both her parents, Sylvia was an emotional wreck, and Garry was her rock, always in control of his emotions.

Hearing him cry did something to Sylvia. As angry and disappointed as she was, instead of her first instinct being *he's getting exactly what he deserves*, Sylvia felt something totally different. She slowly walked down the hallway and into their bedroom.

"Are you okay?" she asked him softly. Even though her voice was barely above a whisper, she could tell that she startled him.

Garry quickly wiped his eyes and cleared his throat and nodded. "I'm good."

"Garry—" Sylvia began, but stopped when she heard the front door open.

"You can take those bags into the kitchen, Nelle. But wait. Give me that Target bag." Aunt Connie's loud voice drifted from downstairs. "Oh, and where is that bag with the stuff for the gumbo in it?"

Sylvia heard her sister answer, "It's still in the trunk. I'll go get it in a second."

"Do you want me to make yours with the andouille sausage or the other kind?"

"Andouille. But I don't think Sylvia eats pork anymore," Janelle told her.

"She sure enough ate them pork chops I fried last week. As a matter of fact, I think she had two. She thinks I don't know that she came back in here and ate them later that night." Aunt Connie laughed.

Sylvia rolled her eyes at no one and shook her head. She glanced over at Garry, who had a smirk on his face. She was busted, because she had sneaked down into the kitchen after everyone was asleep and gotten one of her aunt's amazing fried pork chops. But she only had one. Garry must have eaten the other one, because shortly after she came back upstairs and climbed into bed, he went downstairs.

"Jordan, go help Janelle get those bags out the trunk for me," Aunt Connie yelled. After a few seconds, she yelled again. "Jordan!"

"She's not here!" Sylvia bellowed, causing Garry to jump again.

"I'll go help," he quickly said and rushed out the door.

Sylvia was tempted to call out after him, asking him to wait because she needed to talk. Instead, she sat on the side of the bed and began to pray. She wanted to do the right thing, feel the right thing, believe the right thing, and right now, she didn't know what to do, what she felt, or what she believed. It was her turn to cry.

"Syl?" There was a soft knock at the door. "Are you all right?"

She looked up and saw Janelle standing in the doorway, looking stylish as usual in leggings, a sweater, and a pair of Uggs with a Burberry scarf tied around her neck. Although she was still thick and curvy, it was obvious that Janelle had lost weight and toned up some. Although they both shared their father's dark cocoa complexion and keen nose, Janelle looked more like their mother with her long eyelashes and thick brows. Her sister was beautiful, outgoing, smart, and confident, which made Sylvia wonder why she settled when it came to her love life. It made no sense at all.

"I'm good." Sylvia wiped her tears and used the same words Garry had used moments before.

"No, you're not. And I don't blame you. There's no way you can be good with all of this. I know you don't want to talk to me about it. I understand why, and that's fine. I just need for you to know that I love you and I'm here for you."

Sylvia turned and nodded at her sister. "I'm fine, really. But I appreciate you saying that. Thank you."

"You don't have to thank me, Syl. I'm your sister. I hate that this is even happening to you."

Sylvia knew Janelle was sincere in what she was saying, but the fact still remained that her sister had been sleeping with another woman's husband and still maintained a relationship with him. Sylvia thought it was hypocritical in a sense. She loved her and knew that she meant well, but she didn't feel comfortable talking about it with her. How could she?

"I know you do."

"I'm glad to see you and Garry fighting through this together. I was talking to Aunt Connie, and she said you know love is real when you find the person worth fighting for and who will fight with you. What you and Garry have is real. I've watched the two of you over the past twenty years grow and build together, and I think—no, I know your marriage is worth fighting for."

"Don't you want that?" Sylvia asked her.

"What?" Janelle gave her a confused look and tilted her head to the side.

"Something worth fighting for. Someone to grow and build with," Sylvia said.

Janelle's eyes met hers, and Sylvia saw her body stiffen.

"This isn't about me right now." Janelle frowned.

"Answer the question." Sylvia was not backing down. She'd been wanting to have this conversation with her sister for a while now, and it was time.

"I am fine," Janelle said.

"I didn't say you weren't. I asked if that was something that you wanted. Because I don't think you realize that's what you deserve."

"Sylvia, please don't go there," Janelle pleaded.

"I have to go there. What you're doing is wrong!"

The tension between the two of them grew.

"I'm not doing anything!"

"You are in a relationship with a married man. You don't think that's wrong? Being a side piece?" Sylvia finally said the words she'd been holding back.

"Sylvia, I am *friends* with a man who happens to be married. And the crazy part about all of this is that until this shit went down with Garry, you had no problem with me being friends with Titus. As a matter of fact, I recall you asking me on more than one occasion if I had seen or talked to him, and to tell him you said hello. Oh, wait. What about a couple of months ago when Titus called while you and I were having lunch, and you asked me to pass you the phone? You and him laughed and chatted it up about old times and how you thought he was gonna be your brother-in-law one day. Was it oh-so-wrong then? You didn't seem to mind it one bit!"

Sylvia winced at her sister's words. She knew that, in a way, Janelle was right. She had, in a sense, condoned the relationship she had with Titus for the past few years because it somehow seemed harmless. She knew that they shared a bond that few people find, and that maybe they truly were meant to be together, but circumstances separated them.

When Janelle had first told her that she had run into Titus and they had spent time together, Sylvia thought that it was romantic. Now, the tables were turned, and she was dealing with the fact that her husband had a so-called friend outside of their marriage, and it hurt like hell. She didn't want to think of her sister causing someone else that much pain.

"You're right, and I admit I was wrong for being a part of it and encouraging it. But don't you see what you're doing?" Sylvia shook her head.

"No, I don't, because I'm not Miranda, and Titus isn't Garry. It's not the same thing. I'm not some random chick that Titus met *after* he got married. We loved each other way before that, and you know it. But I messed it up. I walked away, and when he tried to fight for me, I pushed him away. I blew my chances of having a life with him.

It's all my fault, and I get that. And I have tried to stop loving him and to stop thinking about him and to live without him, but I can't. And I wish I could, but I can't. So, maybe this is what I deserve and all I'm supposed to have, and I am fine with that, because I would rather have a piece of Titus than have no parts of him at all."

"Then you are really more pathetic than I thought," Sylvia told her.

Janelle walked out without saying anything else. Alone again, Sylvia lay back on her bed and closed her eyes. She hated arguing with her sister, but she knew what she said was right and it was said out of love. The devastation and hurt on Janelle's face let her know that her words cut a little deeper than she had intended, but Sylvia didn't care. Maybe that was what Janelle needed to feel in order to understand the severity of her actions.

"Sylvia, are you all right?"

Sylvia looked at Garry, and for some reason, she started to laugh. He looked at her strangely until she said, "That seems to be the question of the day, huh?"

"I guess so." He shrugged.

"Is Jordan back?" she asked him.

"Not yet. I'm giving her a little more time to cool off. She'll be back soon. It normally takes her about forty-five minutes and she's good." He sighed, looking overwhelmed.

"So, she does this often?"

"Not really, but she does have a temper. Always has. Walking away is her way of coping, I guess. When she was little and couldn't have her way, she would go into her room and sit in the dark. Her mother felt that it was better than throwing a temper tantrum. You know I wasn't too happy about allowing her to do that, but she made the point that everyone deals with anger in their own way," Garry told her.

Sylvia listened intently as her husband spoke of Jordan and Miranda casually. She searched his face for some sort of clue or sign to indicate the level of their relationship, but there was none. There was only hurt and confusion, which were the same emotions that she was feeling. She thought about the letter Miranda wrote her and came up with the only plan she knew that would get her to the bottom of this.

"When did—" Sylvia started, but Garry interrupted her before she could ask her question.

"Sylvia, I know you want me out of here and I understand why. God knows I put you in an impossible situation. I don't even know what either one of us was thinking when we even agreed to have Jordan come here. No, erase that. I know what I was thinking. I was thinking that it was just like my wife to allow this child that she had no idea even existed into our home. You are such a good woman, and your heart has always been in the right place, and for that I'm grateful. As a matter of fact, I am eternally grateful that you are even giving it a chance.

"But I know this isn't a healthy environment for any of us right now. It's too much stress and tension, and I hate living like this. I love you and Peyton, and even Jordan too much to allow it to continue. It's not fair to any of you. So, I found a place, and it'll be ready in a couple of weeks. Jordan and I are—"

"Wait, Garry." Sylvia hoped and prayed that what she was about to say wasn't something she would live to regret. She decided that it was the only chance their marriage would ever have.

"Hear me out. You're right. Maybe I was a little hasty when I agreed to have Jordan move in here. But I said yes. It was a decision we made as a family. And living here has been trying on all of us. I think part of the problem is that we haven't talked like we need to."

"I tried talking to you, Sylvia."

"I know you have. I was angry, and I still am. I wasn't ready to hear what you had to say. I guess we all deal with anger in our own way," she told him. "But now I'm ready. We need to go to counseling, as a couple and as a family. I'm not saying this will save our marriage. Hell, I don't even know if this is survivable."

"Our marriage is far from over, Sylvia. That thought wasn't even in my head. There is no damn way I'm losing you and my family. It's survivable because I can't survive without you. So, whatever you need me to do, whatever we need to do, I will do it." Garry walked over and kneeled in front of her and took her hands into his.

She stared at her handsome husband as he pleaded with her. Her mind told her heart not to melt. Not yet. It wasn't time.

She maintained her composure and said, "Tell me about Miranda, from beginning to end. I want to know everything, and I mean each and every detail. That's all I want to hear. It's a start, for now."

Garry leaned back and took a deep breath. "I'll tell you everything."

"And, Garry, if you lie or leave out one single detail, this marriage is over."

Sylvia had memorized each and every detail of the letter from Miranda. If what Garry told her matched what Miranda had said, she'd know that as hard as telling the truth was, he loved her enough to be honest. In her mind, she put on her boxing gloves and prepared for what would be the fight for their marriage. Whether they would win had yet to be determined.

Janelle

By the time she left Sylvia's house, Janelle's slight headache was a full-blown migraine. Here she was trying to reach out to her sister and show support, and instead, Sylvia snapped on her. As she drove out of Sylvia's neighborhood, she spotted Jordan walking down the street and pulled over beside her.

"Jordan!"

Jordan glanced over and looked confused. "Yes?"

"It's me, Janelle."

"Oh, hi," Jordan said.

"Where are you going? Your dad is looking for you, and so is Aunt—um . . . yeah, Aunt Connie." At first Janelle didn't know what the girl called their aunt, but then she figured everyone called her Aunt Connie, whether they were related or not.

"I'm going back in a little while," Jordan told her.

"Do you need a ride?" Janelle offered.

"No, I'm good. Thanks." She shook her head.

"Are you sure?" Janelle asked her. Although Sylvia and Garry lived in a prestigious, gated community, she still didn't feel comfortable with the idea of a fifteen-year-old girl walking out alone. Crazy comes in all zip codes and economic levels, according to Aunt Connie. However, her head was hurting, and she didn't want to become any more involved with Sylvia and her household issues than she already was—and her sister had made it clear that she didn't want her around.

"Yeah."

"Well, at least call your father and let him know you're okay," she told her.

"I will." Jordan nodded and continued walking down the street.

Janelle waited a few more moments and then pulled away. She watched Jordan in her rearview mirror until she couldn't see her anymore.

Turning her radio up, she tried to relax and forget about arguing with her sister. Just as she was about to pass the gas station right outside of her neighborhood, she decided to stop and get something for her head. She pulled into the parking lot and parked beside a silver Mercedes. Just as she was about to get out of the car, she spotted Sherrod coming out of the store, talking on his cell phone. She knew it was almost six o'clock, and she wondered exactly what time he was meeting Nivea for drinks. Dressed in a pair of jeans, a Vanderbilt University T-shirt, and some Nike sneakers, he definitely wasn't wearing what she would call date attire, especially not to Jasper's, one of their favorite spots.

"Hey," she said.

He glanced up and looked at her strangely, then put the phone down. "Hey, you. What are you doing on this side of town?"

"Leaving my sister's house."

"Is something wrong? You look like you've been crying." He stepped closer to her, and she could smell the scent of his John Varvatos cologne, which she loved.

"I have a slight headache," she told him. "I'll be all right."

"Okay, feel better," he told her.

"Thanks." She waved and went into the store. While inside, she glanced up and saw him sitting in the Benz she had parked beside. He was a nice guy, good looking and decent. Nivea may just have gotten a winner.

When she walked out, he was still sitting there on his cell phone. She got into her car and left. By the time she got home, she was exhausted and didn't feel well at all. She took a long, hot shower and climbed into bed.

Just as she drifted off to sleep, her phone rang.

"Get dressed and let's go!" Nivea told her.

"What? I am in the bed. I don't feel good. Besides, I thought you had a date with Sherrod," she groaned.

"He flaked out on me. Called and said something came up and he couldn't make it. So now I'm all dressed up with nothing and no one to do." Nivea sighed.

"Were you planning on doing *him*? So soon?" Janelle asked, curious about whether that was what Nivea and Sherrod had planned all along.

"I don't know. Maybe, maybe not. You know you never can tell with me." Nivea laughed.

Janelle knew her best friend was telling the truth. Nivea was an extremist, and when it came to men, there was no method to her madness. Some guys had to wait her out for months to even get a glimpse at the goodies, and others got a sample on the first date. It truly depended on how she felt. She was a free spirit who lived by her own rules, and Janelle had given up on trying to figure her out a long time ago.

A wave of nausea overcame her, and she quickly told Nivea she had to go. She barely made it into the bathroom and over the commode, where she threw up repeatedly. Beads of sweat formed on her head, and she was hot. She slowly crawled back into bed and pulled the covers over her. It was going to be a long night.

It was official; Janelle was sick. She rarely got ill, but not even the taste of Aunt Connie's homemade seafood gumbo was enough to get her out of bed. She spent all day Sunday traveling between her bed and her bathroom. She was miserable. On Monday morning, she called her boss and told him she was dying and wouldn't be making it into the office. He told her he hoped she felt better soon and he would check on her in a couple of days.

By Monday afternoon, she mustered up enough strength to get to the urgent care doctor's office, where they confirmed that she indeed had the dreaded flu and called in a prescription to the pharmacy. She went straight home to what was now the safest place on earth to her—her bed.

She thought she was dreaming when her home phone rang. No one ever called her on it unless it was an emergency.

"Hello," she moaned.

"How are you feeling?" a male voice asked.

She tried to figure out who it was, but she didn't recognize it. "Who is this?"

"This is your friendly neighborhood pharmacist calling to check on you."

"Sherrod?" Her voice perked up a bit, but she still sounded like a man.

"Do you have another friendly pharmacist?" he asked.

She smiled slightly. "No, not one that stalks me like you do. How did you know I was sick?"

"I filled the meds your doc called in. I was waiting for you to come and pick them up, but you didn't. We're closing up, and I wanted to know if you want me to drop them off," he said.

"Closing? What time is it?" she asked, trying to see the time on her phone.

"Almost ten."

Janelle hadn't realized it was that late. When she got home from the doctor, her intentions were to sleep until about six, then get up to go to the store. She checked her cell phone and saw that she had missed several calls, mostly from her aunt and Nivea, both of whom she knew were checking on her.

"I didn't realize it was that late. Thanks, but you don't have to," Janelle told him.

"Are you sure? You're not gonna feel any better until you take them, and I'm pretty sure you need them. I don't mind, and it's on my way home," he offered.

"If you don't mind, I would appreciate it," she said, relieved that she wouldn't have to leave the house.

"I'll be there in about thirty minutes," Sherrod told her.

"Okay," Janelle said. She sat up, telling herself that at least she had time to take a shower before Sherrod got there, but when she stood up, she felt dizzy and quickly sat back down. She hoped she would have enough energy to make it down the steps of her condo to open the door when he arrived.

A little while later, she heard the ringing of her door-bell. Dressed in an oversized T-shirt, some sweatpants, and socks, she wrapped herself up in a blanket and slowly made it downstairs.

"Whoa," he said when she opened the door. He had several bags in his hands, along with a small bouquet of flowers.

Janelle knew if she looked anything like she felt, then it was pretty bad—but she didn't care. "Come in."

Sherrod followed her inside and down the hallway into the living room. Janelle plopped down on the sofa and fell to the side. The trip from her bedroom, downstairs, then into her living room had taken every bit of her energy, and she felt like she was dying.

"Well, I guess I don't need to ask how you're feeling." Sherrod laughed. "Where is your kitchen?"

"To your right," she answered, her head still slumped on the arm of her sofa. "And I'm glad you find this so amusing."

"Hey, I don't really feel bad. I recall offering you a flu shot on three different occasions, and you declined. You said you *never* get the flu," he reminded her.

"I don't. You did this to me. Admit it," Janelle moaned. She could hear the opening and closing of her refrigerator and cabinets and the sound of ice being placed in a glass. Any other time she would be worried that there was a strange man she barely knew in her kitchen, but she could only hope and pray that Sherrod didn't turn out to be a serial rapist and she wouldn't end up as inspiration for a new episode of *Law and Order SVU*. She leaned and stretched her arm, reaching for the coffee table. Grabbing the remote to the television, she turned it on, hoping to catch a rerun of *Real Housewives of Atlanta*. Within a few minutes, she dozed off again.

"Come on, sit up for a minute." Sherrod's voice woke her up.

She glanced up and saw that he was standing in front of her, holding a baking sheet that he had turned into a makeshift tray. On it was a bowl of soup, a steaming cup of tea, a glass of orange juice, and a bottle of water, none of which were in her kitchen prior to his arrival.

"You need to drink, because I know you're dehydrated, and you need to try and eat a little something before you take these meds."

Janelle sat up and stared at him as he set the tray on the coffee table in front of her. He gently touched her forehead, and she shuddered as a chill went down her spine. She didn't know if it was because she was feverish or because of how gentle his touch was.

"You didn't have to do all of this," she whispered.

"I know. But I also know how sick you are if your doctor called in all these meds, and when you didn't come pick them up, I was worried about you. What do you wanna drink first?" he asked.

Janelle looked at her choices and said, "Water."

He opened the bottle of VOSS water and passed it to her.

She took a long swallow, nearly drinking the entire bottle in one swig. "Oh my God, that was the best water I ever had."

"Here, eat this." He passed her the bowl of soup. "Careful, it's hot."

Janelle looked into the bowl and was pleased to see it was chicken and rice, her favorite. She slowly took a few spoonfuls and savored the taste as it went down her throat.

"It's good," she said, taking a few more bites.

"I'm glad you like it. I take pride in my culinary skills." He gave himself a slight pat on the chest.

"Don't you mean your can opening skills?" She giggled.

"I'm gonna let that one pass because you're ill," he told her. He reached on the table and took the remote, changing the channels just as NeNe Leakes was yelling on the screen. "Why do you watch this ridiculousness?"

"It's not ridiculous; it's entertainment. What do you call this?" Janelle asked, referring to SportsCenter, which was now playing on the TV.

"This is educational and informative," Sherrod said matter-of-factly.

"It's the same stuff over and over. The scores aren't gonna change," she said between spoonfuls of soup.

"It's not just about the scores, woman. It's much more than that," he told her.

"Whatever." Janelle placed her now empty bowl back on the tray. She felt a little better, but she was still exhausted. Just as she was about to lay back down, he stopped her.

"Time for meds," Sherrod said as he opened the bottles and poured the pills into her hand one by one. "This one is definitely gonna make you sleepy, but you won't be nauseous anymore, especially now that you've eaten."

"Good, but trust me, I can't sleep any harder than I've been sleeping the past two days," she told him.

"We'll see if you say that tomorrow when you wake up." He passed her the juice, and she drank it.

"You're such a nice guy," she said and sat back on the sofa.

Sherrod took the glass away from her, and then he stood up, clearing up her mess. He left the water and the tea for her on the table.

"I try to be. You need anything else?" he asked.

"No, everything is perfect," she mumbled. Her eyes were getting heavy, and she pulled the blanket around her as she lay back. The last thing she remembered was hearing that annoying SportsCenter theme song.

When she woke up, Sherrod was gone, NeNe and the other housewives of Atlanta were back on her television, and the bouquet of flowers was in a small vase on the table beside her bottle of water, along with several women's' magazines and tabloids. The bottles of medicine were also there, and on a piece of paper, specific instructions about how to take them, handwritten by Sherrod, including his phone number. He told her to call if she needed anything else.

He is a really nice guy, Janelle thought as she looked at the note, smiling.

Sylvia

"Are you going to be able to make the appointment this afternoon?" Sylvia asked Garry as she made the bed. He was in the sitting area of the bedroom where he still slept nightly. They had been making an effort to communicate better, especially since, as far as she could tell, he was being honest.

"Just let me know where and what time," Garry told her. "I will be there."

She thought back to days ago, when they had come to the crossroads that they were now at. Later that night, after Jordan had come back home and been disciplined, and everyone had finally gone into their rooms, she and Garry sat down across from one another and talked.

"Where did you meet her?" Sylvia had asked. She figured this would be a great place to start, especially since it was where Miranda had started in the letter.

Garry took a deep breath and closed his eyes momentarily. When he opened them, he looked at her and said, "We met at a funeral home."

"A funeral home?" Sylvia frowned. Miranda said the two met at a time of great sadness for both of them, but she hadn't mentioned a funeral home.

"Yes, I was making arrangements for my father; she was making arrangements for her fiancé, who was killed during an armed robbery."

"You told me you didn't know your father," Sylvia said.

"I didn't. But for some reason, when he died, I was located as his next of kin. So, I had to make the arrangements." He looked down at the floor.

"Why didn't you tell me?" Sylvia frowned at him.

"Because you had just lost—we had . . . I mean, your father, then your mother, and then . . . you had already dealt with enough, Syl. I didn't want to add anything else for you to deal with. It would've been too much," he said, slowly shaking his head.

Sylvia already knew what he meant. She had done her own calculating in her head as she read the letter and come to the realization that Miranda and Garry met weeks after she suffered a miscarriage. She couldn't stop the tears from forming in her eyes even if she wanted to. Garry reached out for her hand, and she quickly pulled it back.

"Go ahead, keep talking," she told him. This wasn't the time for his affection or comfort; it was time for his honesty. She wanted both of them to focus on the subject at hand.

"I mean, that's where we met. It was the weirdest thing, because I was the only family that my father had, and she felt bad because I was all alone, so we talked. The services for both of them were at the same time, right across the hall from one another. A month later, I went back to Drakesville to take care of some final paperwork. I went into this bar, and she was there. We talked and had some drinks—well, a whole lot of drinks, and I went home with her. I know, I know, it's so cliché, and I know being drunk is no excuse for what I did. But it happened. I really don't even remember having sex with her. I just remember putting on my clothes and leaving her apartment."

Sylvia continued to listen. So far, what he was saying was what Miranda had explained in her letter, somewhat. She allowed Garry to continue.

"A few months later, she called me and told me she was pregnant. When she told me, I thought she was just sharing her news, until she told me that there was a possibility that I was the father. I swear, I was confused and didn't know what to do." Garry finally looked up at her.

"You should have told me," Sylvia whispered.

"I didn't know how. I couldn't. I thought about it, but I just couldn't. In my mind, I loved you too much, and I knew it would break your heart. And I didn't want to risk doing that until I knew for sure that I was indeed the father. I decided to wait and see." He blinked, then looked down again.

"When did you find out? Because you're in the pictures with Jordan when she was born." Sylvia waited for his answer. She wondered if Garry had been in the delivery room with Miranda, holding her hand and encouraging her to push the same way he had been by her side when she delivered Peyton. The thought of him sharing that intimate moment with someone other than her was enough to crush her, and she wondered if she was going to be able to handle the truth now that she had asked him for it.

"I went to the hospital the day after she was born. One look at Jordan and Miranda knew she had to be mine," he said.

Hearing that he hadn't been there when Miranda had the baby made her feel a little better. Childbirth was an experience he'd only shared with her. She remembered seeing the pictures of a newborn Jordan and told him, "She looks just like you."

"Miranda knew that I was in a terrible position. She knew how much you and Peyton meant to me, and how much I loved and valued my family. We agreed that I would be a father and a provider for Jordan, and when the time was right, I would tell you. The time just never seemed to be right," Garry said.

"Did you ever sleep with her again?" Again, Sylvia asked one of the questions she wasn't sure she wanted to know the answers to, and she held her breath as she waited for Garry's response.

"Never. I never even spent the night. Miranda and I were co-parents, and, I admit, we were friends. She didn't have much family of her own other than Jordan and me. She remained close with her fiancé's brother, but that's about it. Her focus was all about Jordan. She doted on her and spoiled her rotten, but she was a great mom," he told her.

Sylvia knew that Miranda was a good mom. Garry confirmed everything that she had written in the letter. The fact that she praised Garry as a father and a provider came as no surprise to her. He prided himself on being everything that his father wasn't.

"Is there anything else you need to tell me? Is there anything else I need to know?"

"Yes," Garry told her. "You need to know that I love you, and I'm sorry that I didn't tell you. I never did any of this to hurt you. I appreciate you, and I know the same way you don't deserve any of this, I don't deserve you, but I am not going to lose you."

"Is that it?" She peered at him.

"That's it." He nodded emphatically.

They stood up and stared at one another. Garry slowly took a step toward her and took her by the hand. This time, she didn't pull away. Instead, she allowed him to take her into his arms and hold her tight. At first, she remained still, unmoving in his tight embrace. Then, she felt something stir within and allowed herself to enjoy the security of her husband's body. Her arms wrapped around him, and she buried her head in his chest and cried, releasing all of the emotions she had been holding within. As he held her tight, whispering how much he loved her, she glanced up and saw that he was crying too. It was then that she realized that she was not in this fight alone.

"I will text you the address for the therapist," she told him and walked out of the bedroom.

She walked down the hallway and was about to knock on Peyton's door to make sure she was ready for school when she was shocked to hear what sounded like a man talking.

"You know that was mad funny, yo," the voice said.

"It wasn't. I was so embarrassed when you did that." Peyton laughed.

"I wasn't trying to embarrass you. I was trying to make you smile."

Sylvia hesitated, and then gently opened the door, popping her head inside. "Peyton?"

"Mom!" Peyton jumped, then quickly closed the laptop that was in her lap.

"Who is in here?" Sylvia looked around her daughter's room, searching for the owner of the deep voice, but she didn't find anyone.

"No one, Mom. Why are you just coming in here like this?" Peyton snapped. She stood up and grabbed her uniform sweater off the bed and put it on.

"Who were you talking to?" Sylvia asked, wondering who was causing her daughter's sudden nervous behavior.

"Nobody, Mom." Peyton's voice was an entire octave higher than normal.

"Peyton, I'm not crazy. I heard you talking and laughing with a boy. Now, who was it?" Sylvia folded her arms and waited for Peyton's answer.

"Just a friend, that's all. It's not that serious."

"It must be serious. Whatever you were talking about couldn't wait until you got to school," Sylvia said.

"He doesn't even go to my school." Peyton put the laptop on her desk and picked up her backpack. "Come on. I don't want to be late."

"He doesn't go to your school? What school does he go to? Who is this boy, Peyton?" Sylvia was now more curious than concerned. She was also a little disappointed that Peyton felt the need to hide whomever her so-called friend was. She'd always thought her daughter would feel comfortable enough to come to her when she was ready to date, but then again, she thought she knew her husband well enough to know if he'd had an affair.

Guess I was wrong on both accounts, she thought to herself.

"His name is Tank. He goes to Coastal, and we're just friends." Peyton sighed.

Coastal High School was the public school that Jordan attended. Sylvia wondered if she knew this mystery boy as well.

"Peyton, I'm not making a big deal out of anything. You're a beautiful seventeen-year-old girl. I would be making a big deal out of it if you didn't have male friends. But I'm still your mother, and I still need and want to know who this friend is, and I'm sure your father would like to as well," she told her daughter.

Peyton looked at her mother in horror. "No, Mom! No way! You know how Daddy is. Please, don't. I swear, if it gets serious, I will tell you."

"It doesn't have to be serious, Peyton. Even if he's just a friend, we still want to meet him." Sylvia gave her daughter a reassuring smile. "I promise you, if I didn't love and care about you, I wouldn't even be concerned about who you talk to."

She wasn't exaggerating when she said Peyton was beautiful. Even in the plaid skirt and white blouse that Peyton had worn to school daily for the past eleven years, Sylvia could see the womanly curves that she had developed. She was grateful that in addition to inheriting her father's good looks and athletic ability, her daughter had also inherited the same curves that Janelle had from her mother. It was a perfect combination to look at for an adolescent boy, and Sylvia knew Peyton probably got a lot of attention that she probably didn't even realize. When it came to personality, their daughter was more like her mother: shy, quiet, and naïve when it came to boys.

"Fine, Mom. Come on. We're gonna be late, and I have a yearbook meeting this morning."

They went downstairs and into the kitchen where Aunt Connie and Jordan were having breakfast already.

"Good morning," Sylvia greeted them.

"Good morning," Jordan mumbled, barely looking up from the iPhone she was texting on.

"Good morning. The bacon and grits are on the stove. And before you ask: no, it ain't turkey bacon, it's pork. You want your eggs scrambled or fried?" Aunt Connie got up and walked over to the stove.

"Just coffee and I'm good, Aunt Connie." Sylvia shook her head.

"Are these homemade?" Peyton asked, picking up one of the golden, fluffy biscuits that were sitting on a plate in the middle of the table.

"Of course. You know they ain't come out of no can." Aunt Connie laughed.

"They are amazing!" Peyton told her. "I just want one of these with some bacon and grape jelly, Aunt Connie."

"I don't know why I made all these grits if y'all ain't gonna eat 'em." Aunt Connie passed Peyton a plate of bacon.

"You know Garry will eat them," Sylvia said, walking over to her Keurig to make a cup of coffee.

"I already made a pot of coffee." Aunt Connie pointed to the dripping machine in the corner. "And it's good."

Sylvia gave up on trying to explain to her aunt that the Keurig allowed the family to have a variety of flavored coffees, hot chocolate, and tea. She had showed her several times how simple the machine was to use, but her aunt refused and insisted on using the old-fashioned Mr. Coffee machine and Maxwell House coffee every morning. Sylvia also knew that the comment about the canned biscuits was a dig at her as well, because on the rare occasion that her Aunt Connie allowed her to make breakfast, the only biscuits she made were the ones with the Pillsbury Dough Boy on the label.

"Daddy does love grits. He messes them up, though, with all that sugar he puts in 'em, and cinnamon." Peyton laughed.

"Yes, he does," Sylvia agreed. "I've told him for years they're grits, not cream of wheat or oatmeal. The only thing you're supposed to put in grits is salt, pepper, and butter!"

She and Peyton laughed together.

"Oh, there's nothing wrong with a little variety," Aunt Connie told them. "You know he's from Chicago. It's a Northern thing. Isn't that right, Jordan?"

Sylvia looked over and saw that Jordan was now staring at them, her face void of any signs of amusement.

"I'm gonna be late for the bus," Jordan said, getting up from the table.

"Jordan, I can give you a ride to school if you like. It's not a problem," Sylvia offered.

"That's okay," Jordan replied. "I like to ride the bus to school. It's a *Northern thing*."

The room remained quiet for a few seconds until Sylvia finally spoke. "I give up. Each time I try, she shuts me out. I don't even know what that was about."

"Me neither." Peyton shrugged, slathering jelly onto her biscuit.

"Maybe you two should be a little more observant then." Aunt Connie pointed to Jordan's plate, which was still on the table. On the plate was a half-eaten biscuit, bits of bacon, and uneaten grits, with cinnamon and sugar on top.

Sylvia realized what her aunt meant, and even though it was harmless, she knew how their jovial conversation must've made Jordan feel. Once again, they'd isolated her.

Janelle

"Well, well, well. Look who's feeling better."

"Yes, I'm feeling much better." Janelle smiled at Sherrod as she looked at him standing behind the glass casing of the area at the rear of the store, dressed in his blue lab coat. He already knew that she was feeling better, because he called and texted her daily to make sure. It was Thursday and the first day she really felt almost one hundred percent and well enough to leave her house. So, she decided to stop by the pharmacy and thank him in person for being so considerate and concerned while she was ill. If it weren't for him, she probably wouldn't have gotten better so quickly.

"I'm glad. You look a hell of a lot better than the last time I saw you, that's for sure." He laughed.

"I'm sure I do, but don't hate, because even on my worst days, I know I still look good," she told him. She had made sure she looked good before she left the house that afternoon. Her hair was curled perfectly, and she had taken the time to make sure her makeup was tight and so was the outfit she wore. As she got dressed, she had convinced herself that the reason she was being so meticulous had nothing to do with her decision to stop by and see him but was because she was, indeed, feeling better.

"I mean, you was a'ight, I guess." He grinned.

There were quite a few customers in the waiting area, some seated and some in line. She didn't want to take up too much of his time.

"I know you're busy. I just wanted to stop by and thank you again."

"Give me a few minutes to get these meds out and we can go talk for a minute," he replied.

"Okay," Janelle said.

In order to both kill time and not stand around idly while he was working, she decided to pick up a few items while she was there. Just as she was about to check out at the front of the store, she heard him behind her.

"Are you sure you don't need to buy any protection while you're here?"

"No, I don't. Are you sure you don't need any? You know what Aunt Connie told you." She smirked at him.

"She told you the same thing," he reminded her.

She noticed the cashier giggling and realized they were holding up the line. She paid for her items and gathered up her bags.

"Let me help you with those. You might still be kinda weak," he said, taking the bags out of her hand. "After all, you were *dying*, as you put it."

"I was dying. People die from the flu every day. I read it on webmd.com," she told him.

"Oh God, please stay off that site." He rolled his eyes, leading her over to the perfume counter where no one was, so they could talk.

"Why? It's informative and insightful."

"Touché." He laughed, placing her bags on the counter. "So, what are you doing for your birthday this weekend?"

Janelle laughed. "How did you know it's my birthday?"

"I know a lot. I'm your friendly neighborhood pharmacist." He pointed to the name tag on the blue lab coat he wore.

"That's kinda scary. Should I be worried?" She squinted in a playful way.

"I don't know. Should you?" The way he said it let her know that he was obviously flirting at this point.

Janelle looked at him, staring. There was something about him that drew her to him, and she wondered how she should respond. Finally, after what felt like an eternity, she said, "I hope not."

"Trust me," he told her. "You shouldn't. So, answer my original question. What do you have planned for your birthday?"

Janelle was worried that her recent illness would prevent her from celebrating her birthday, which was the following Friday night. Nivea had been even more excited than she was when Janelle called to say that she was feeling better and would be well enough to celebrate.

"Nothing much. Girls night on Thursday night, dinner and drinks on Friday night, and brunch with the family on Saturday," Janelle told him.

"Wow, that doesn't sound like much at all." Sherrod shook his head. "So, let me ask you this: does that mean I can take you to dinner on Saturday night?"

Janelle was both surprised and excited by his invitation. In her mind, she had expected that she would do something with Jarvis on Saturday night; although he had mentioned it, they hadn't made any concrete plans. Going on a date with Sherrod sounded like fun, but she was hesitant. She knew that Nivea had mentioned being interested in him.

"Um, dinner? Saturday night?" She blinked.

"Yeah, dinner Saturday night, if you would like to." He stood from where he'd been leaning on the glass counter moments before.

Janelle tried to think of the right thing to say and do. On one hand, she wanted to go and get to know Sherrod. He had really been so nice and done so much for her while she was sick that she felt like she was the one who should have been asking him out to dinner. Now, here he was, asking to take her. On the other hand, agreeing to do so knowing her best friend was interested in him was not right. She was torn and wondered if feeling flattered and having the desire to even want to accept his invitation broke girl code in a way.

"Dr. Crawford, code seventeen. Dr. Crawford, code seventeen." A voice paged Sherrod over the intercom, and Janelle almost let out a sigh of relief.

"Duty calls," Sherrod said, picking the bags up and handing them to her. "Thanks for stopping by to see me. It was a nice surprise."

"You don't have to thank me. I told you I came here to thank you. I appreciate your looking out for me while I was sick and shut in." She smiled at him.

"And on your death bed?" He laughed.

"Exactly."

"Hey, it's what I do. After all, I'm your—"

They both laughed as she finished his sentence for him. "Friendly neighborhood pharmacist."

"Well, let me know about dinner. I work Saturday until five," he told her. "I would love to take you out and celebrate. After all, you almost didn't make it."

"I will," Janelle told him, taking her bags from him and watching him walk away.

"Happy birthday, Nellie!" Nivea screamed as Janelle made her way through the crowd and over to the bar where she, Natalie, and a few other friends were already waiting.

"Thank you! Thank you!" Janelle went over and hugged them. It was the start of her celebration weekend, and she was ready to party. She only had two more years to enjoy her thirties, and she decided that thirty-eight was going to be an age to remember, although she didn't have everything she thought she would have by this age—such as: a husband or children, or, hell, even a committed relationship. She still had a lot to celebrate because she had a decent job, a home, her family, friends, and her health.

They immediately ordered a round of tequila shots. Janelle didn't have to work the next day, but because she was just getting over the flu and on antibiotics, she knew to take it easy and not get too "turnt up."

She was having a great time with her girls when, all of a sudden, she looked up and Jarvis was walking toward her.

"Surprise!" Nivea screamed.

Janelle turned to her friend and said, "What the hell? I thought this was girls' night."

"I know, but I figured you hadn't seen him since you've been sick, so I texted him and told him we were gonna be here." Nivea beamed with pride.

The first thing that ran through Janelle's mind was how in the world did Nivea know Jarvis's cell phone number? But she decided to ask that question at a later time.

Jarvis walked up to her and gave her a hug and kissed her on the cheek. "Happy birthday." He smiled.

"Thank you." Janelle smiled back, admiring how handsome he looked. She was glad to see him and enjoyed the fact that he came out on a weeknight, something he rarely did.

"Bartender, another round!" Nivea said.

The bartender lined up more shot glasses in front of them.

"What is that?" Jarvis asked.

"Cuervo!" Nivea told him.

"Oh, no, I'm good. I just want a beer. I gotta work tomorrow." He laughed.

"Aw, come on. Don't be like that, Jarvis. It's your girl's birthday." Nivea put her arm around Janelle.

Jarvis hated being the center of attention. She knew her best friend was tipsy, and if she didn't curtail the situation, there was a possibility of Nivea making Jarvis feel even more uncomfortable than he already looked.

"Can I get a Heineken please?" Janelle leaned over and asked the bartender.

"Coming right up," the bartender said and quickly returned with the cold beer, which Janelle passed to Jarvis.

"Thanks, sweetie." He smiled, and she was glad to see him loosen up a bit.

They all continued to laugh and joke with one another, and the DJ began playing a mix of Mary J. Blige, who happened to be Janelle's favorite artist of all time. Jarvis pulled her to the dance floor, and she swayed to the beat of everything from "Real Love" to "Just Fine."

Janelle was enjoying the moment when she looked up and saw Nivea walking onto the dance floor, pulling Sherrod behind her. Their eyes met, and for an instant, she stood completely still. He had a mischievous grin, and she forced herself to look away.

"Look who decided to come out, Nellie!" Nivea yelled over the music.

"Happy birthday, lady!" Sherrod smiled.

"Thank you," Janelle said. The music slowed and changed to "My Life," and Jarvis pulled her close to him. She hoped he couldn't feel her heart pounding.

"You look so beautiful," he looked down and whispered. "Were you surprised to see me?"

"Yes, I am," she told him.

"I'm glad I came out. If I hadn't, some other brother would probably be all over you right now." His arms tightened around her body.

She wondered if Jarvis caught the connection between her and Sherrod, but she also wondered if what she was feeling was actually a connection. She looked over at him dancing with Nivea, laughing and whispering in his ear. Again, she felt a slight discomfort that she knew was jealousy.

"You know that's not true." She refocused her attention back to her dance partner.

"It is. When I walked in, there were two dudes checking you out," Jarvis told her.

"What? Where are they?" Janelle teased, pretending like she was looking around the club for the men Jarvis was talking about.

"Stop it," Jarvis said.

They danced a little while longer and then went back over to the bar.

Jarvis looked at his watch and said, "Well, I gotta get outta here."

"I really appreciate you coming out, Jarvis." She smiled as she put her arms around his neck.

"I was flattered that your friends thought enough about me to invite me out here. I had a great time," he told her.

"Me too," she said, looking back over to the dance floor at Nivea and Sherrod, who also seemed to be having the time of their lives. Jarvis gave her a hug and another kiss on the cheek.

"Text me to let me know you made it home safely. Happy birthday," he said as he released her from his arms.

"Thank you," Janelle said.

When he was gone, she took her seat at the bar and ordered a ginger ale to ease the queasiness in her stomach, which she now felt. She hoped she hadn't rushed her recovery and her flu was returning.

"Where's Jarvis?" Natalie leaned over and asked.

"He left. You know he has to work tomorrow," she told her.

"We do too. He is so boring." Natalie laughed. "You need someone fun, like Kenny. That's who we should've invited. I told Nivea to tell him to come out."

"Oh, my goodness. I keep telling you Kenny is a man whore." Janelle laughed and shook her head.

"That's the kind I like!" Natalie winked, and they fell out laughing.

"What's so funny?" Nivea came back to the bar, followed by Sherrod. "Where's your boo?"

Janelle's eyes widened at Nivea's question, and she blushed while avoiding looking at Sherrod. It was bad enough that Jarvis had been a little more touchy-feely than he normally was in public. She was sure Sherrod probably thought they really were a couple, which they weren't.

"He left. You know it was past his bedtime." Natalie giggled.

"Why? It's not even your birthday yet! He couldn't wait twenty more minutes?" Nivea asked, pointing to her watch.

Janelle just shrugged.

"See, that's why I told you to invite Kenny! He would still be here!" Natalie told her.

"Dang, girl, how many boos you got?" Sherrod teased.

"Kenny's not her boo. That's her sister's business partner and our friend," Nivea explained to him.

"I'm trying to make Kenny my boo!" Natalie nodded.

"I tried calling and texting Kenny," Nivea said. "He didn't reply."

"You shoulda told him you wanted to give him some ass. I guarantee he would've called you back immediately." Janelle laughed.

"Probably," Nivea agreed.

They ordered another round of shots, and Sherrod held his glass up. "Well, folks, it's midnight. To the birthday girl!"

They joined him and clinked glasses, wishing Janelle a happy birthday and well wishes.

Janelle felt the vibration of her cell phone and took it out of her purse. She looked down and saw that there was a text message. It was from Titus.

Happy Birthday to the woman who will always hold my heart. I love you.

Just as she was about to respond to the text, Sherrod grabbed her by the hand and pulled her onto the dance floor.

"What are you doing?" she hissed, nearly dropping her phone.

"Dancing with the birthday girl. What's the problem? Is your *man* gonna get mad?" He peered at her. His tone was light, but the way he was looking at her let her know that he really wanted to know the answer.

"That's not my *man*. That's my friend." She made sure to clarify. "I don't have a man."

"Then what's wrong?" He shrugged.

Janelle looked over at Nivea, who was again the center of attention at the bar, talking to some guys. Her friend didn't even seem to notice that Sherrod had pulled her away.

"What?" Sherrod asked, looking confused.

"Nothing," Janelle said, thinking she was making a big deal out of a simple dance.

When the song ended, he pulled her to a nearby empty table in the corner where they sat across from each other.

"Did you decide about dinner yet?" He leaned closer so she could hear him over the music.

Janelle had thought about it, but she hadn't made a decision. She was still trying to figure out if she should mention it to Nivea. She had hoped to say something that night about it, but her plans had been diverted once he walked in.

"I'm still thinking about it," she said slowly.

"Then let me help you decide." He stood up and pulled her body against his, whispering in her ear and touching her softly on the neck. "I will pick you up at seven. Be ready. Happy birthday, Nellie."

Janelle could barely get the word "okay" out of her mouth, so she just nodded.

He walked back to the bar, leaving her all alone, pondering. She watched him briefly hug Nivea and Natalie, and then he looked back at her and waved goodbye.

It's just dinner, she told herself, *that's all*. But somehow, she knew it was going to be much more than that, and she was looking forward to it.

Sylvia

It had been a long but productive Friday. Sylvia had three meetings with Kenny and clients, all of which had gone remarkably well. She had dropped Aunt Connie off at the bingo hall for the afternoon after swinging by the mall, where she picked up a Michael Kors purse with the matching wallet for Janelle's birthday gift. She was now back at home and decided to do something she hadn't done in a long time: relax and take a hot bubble bath in her Jacuzzi tub. She ran the water, put on some music, lit some candles, and submerged herself for nearly an hour. It was some much-needed private time that she truly enjoyed.

When she stepped out of the tub, Sylvia wrapped herself in a towel and walked into her bedroom. She was startled to find Garry standing there, and she screamed.

"What are you doing home?" she asked when she finally caught her breath.

"I . . . because . . ." Garry stuttered but never answered her question.

She could feel his eyes traveling along her body, and she pulled the towel tighter around her, suddenly conscious of her nakedness. She could see the wanting in his eyes, and she turned her back to him. She could still hear music coming from the bathroom.

"Syl," Garry called her name.

Sylvia looked at his reflection in the mirror of their dresser and saw him walk toward her. She didn't move when she felt his body behind hers, and she didn't know who was more surprised, him or her. It had been weeks since she had felt his touch, and she missed it. She continued to stare as he tilted his head and kissed her neck, reaching for the towel and pulling it off. She let it drop to the floor and arched her back, reaching for his hands and putting them on her breasts. He played with her hardened nipples, and his kisses continued down her back. He turned her around, and they stared at one another. She pulled his head to her and kissed him passionately. She had missed everything about him, but his kiss had been what she missed most of all. It was soft, wet, hot and inviting—everything that she felt when she was with him.

He lifted her off the ground and carried her to their bed, gently placing her down. They both fumbled to take his clothes off, and then he paused. At first, Sylvia thought something was wrong, until she saw Garry smiling at her. Just as she was about to ask what he was doing, he put his finger on her lips to silence her, and she listened. She then smiled back at him as she realized what was putting the smile on his face. It was D'Angelo's "Untitled." When the song first came out, the music video used to make Sylvia swoon, and Garry once overheard her comment on how she wanted a "piece of that." That same night, Garry came out of the shower, while making sure that song was on, and took her to a new sexual height. From that moment on, it had been "their song."

Sylvia's heart began pounding, and Garry wrapped his arms around her legs and pulled her to him. She lay back and moaned as he licked her inner thighs and spread her wetness open with his talented tongue. Deeper and deeper he licked, teasing and sucking on her clitoris until she begged him to stop. Garry refused, and she had no other choice but to release as he continued tasting her.

Over and over, he continued to please her orally, until he was satisfied that she'd had enough.

By the time he climbed on top of her, Sylvia had lost count of how many times she came and wondered if she would be able to take any more. Garry guided her hands around his swollen manhood, and she became aroused all over again. She gasped as he entered her, and she enjoyed each and every inch of him. She bit into his shoulder and lifted her hips off the bed to meet his thrust, knowing having her "throw it back on him" was one of the things he loved.

"Tell me you missed this," she demanded.

"Damn, I missed this." He nodded slowly.

"Tell me how much you love it," she continued as her arms reached and grabbed the headboard of their bed.

"I love it," he told her.

"Tell me," she panted.

"I love it, Syl. You know I love it." Garry grunted, his lust-filled eyes staring at her.

"Tell me it's the best."

"It's the best, baby. It's always been the best."

"Prove it," she whispered. "Cum for me."

"No, Syl, not yet," Garry said.

She knew she was almost there, and Garry was too. Once she told him to cum, he couldn't resist. Hearing her tell him was his trigger word, and he damn near lost control every time.

"Cum for me . . . *now*." Sylvia tightened her walls around him and gasped his name. "Garry!"

As if on cue, Garry followed her command and climaxed with her. They were both panting and dripping with sweat as he rolled off of her.

"Damn," he said.

"Why did you come home again?" Sylvia laughed.

"Hell, I don't even remember."

***

Sylvia was still floating from her afternoon of lovemaking when she pulled up to the school to pick up Peyton. She waited for almost twenty minutes for her daughter, and then parked the car and went inside the building. The hallways were fairly empty, but that was normal for a Friday afternoon. Peyton hadn't mentioned any type of meeting or practice when she had dropped her off, so she wondered where she could be. Sylvia walked into the office and asked the secretary.

"No, Mrs. Blackwell, there aren't any activities scheduled today, and I haven't seen Peyton," the woman said.

"Okay, thank you," Sylvia said and walked back to her truck.

She checked her phone, and when she didn't see a text or missed call from Peyton, she tried to reach her. There was no answer. Sylvia dialed Meagan's phone, but she didn't answer either. Sylvia sent both girls a text message and told them to call her back immediately. She then called Meagan's mother, who said Meagan was at work at the mall, but she didn't know where Peyton was. She promised to call Sylvia if she heard anything.

Sylvia tried not to panic, but this was not like her daughter. She wondered if she should call the police. Her phone rang, and thinking it was Peyton, she answered without looking at the caller ID.

"Hello."

"I've been sitting out here waiting on you, child. Did you forget about me?" Aunt Connie asked.

She had forgotten to pick her aunt up from bingo. "I'm on my way, Aunt Connie. I came to pick Peyton up from school, and she's not here. I don't know where she is."

"Calm down. She's probably somewhere with Meagan," Aunt Connie told her.

"Meagan is at work." Sylvia's voice began to tremble.

"Just come and pick me up, and we will go and look for her. I promise you, Peyton is fine. She is a good girl. Now, come on."

"Okay." Sylvia tried to calm down and headed to go pick up her aunt. Again the phone rang, and she quickly answered. "Hello."

"Hey, baby. I want to take you to dinner tonight. You feel like dressing up and going to Copeland's?" Garry asked.

"I don't know, Garry. I can't talk about that right now."

"What's wrong, Syl? What's going on?"

Sylvia didn't want to upset Garry, but she thought he should know, so she told him. "I don't know where Peyton is. She wasn't there when I went to pick her up."

"What? What do you mean? Did you call her?"

Sylvia could hear the anxiousness in her husband's voice.

"Yes, I called and texted her. I am going to go pick Aunt Connie up now, and we are gonna go look for her."

"I'm on my way. I'll meet y'all at the house," Garry said and hung up.

An hour later, there was still no sign of Peyton. Sylvia was beyond worried. She even reached out to Jordan for help.

"Jordan, do you have any idea where Peyton could be?" Sylvia asked her.

"I don't know." Jordan shrugged. "I'm sorry."

"I mean, I know y'all aren't close, but aren't you her friend on Facebook? Don't you all have some mutual friends?"

"We aren't Facebook friends. We follow each other on Instagram, but that's about it."

"Why aren't you friends on Facebook?" Garry asked. "That's your sister. You've been living in the same house for the past month and a half."

"Why are you yelling at me? This isn't my fault." Jordan frowned.

"I'm not yelling!" Garry yelled.

Sylvia looked over at him and nodded. "Yes, you are, Garry. And she's right. It's not her fault."

"I can go look on my page and see if we have any mutual friends or something." Jordan excused herself.

"I'm telling y'all she's fine," Aunt Connie told them.

"Then she needs to let us know that she's fine!" Sylvia said.

Her cell phone rang, and she saw Meagan's face on her caller ID.

"Meagan, where is Peyton?" Sylvia said without even saying hello.

"Aunt Sylvia, I just got your message because I've been at work since after school."

"Does she know where she is? Has she seen her?" Garry asked.

"She's at work, Garry. She hasn't seen Peyton," Sylvia told him. "If she calls or if you hear from her, please let me know. Tell her to call home."

"I will," Meagan told them.

"Maybe we should call the police," Sylvia said.

"No," Aunt Connie said. "The girl ain't even been missing but three hours."

Sylvia walked out of the living room and into the kitchen. It was as if her worst nightmare was coming true. Her daughter had never done anything like this; something had to be wrong. Recent news stories about abducted girls and sex trafficking flashed in her mind, and she became even more panicked. The doorbell rang, and Sylvia rushed to open it, hoping it was Peyton. Instead, she found Janelle standing there.

"Is she home?" her sister asked as she walked into the foyer.

"No," Sylvia told her, her eyes filling up with tears.

Janelle hugged her tight. "Syl, don't cry. She's fine. Peyton is probably somewhere at a college informational seminar that she forgot to tell you about."

"Then why hasn't she contacted us?" Sylvia asked.

"I don't know, but I'm sure there's some sort of good explanation," Janelle said reassuringly.

"I'm gonna go ride around and look for her," Garry told them as he passed where they were talking and headed toward the front door.

"Where?" Sylvia questioned.

"I don't know, but I can't just wait here," he told her.

He opened the door, and to their surprise, there was Peyton.

"Hi, Daddy," she said as if her arriving home three and a half hours late was no problem.

"Don't 'Hi, Daddy' me, Peyton Janelle Blackwell! Get in here! You are in so much trouble!" Garry told her.

Sylvia, no longer able to control her emotions, sobbed and rushed over to Peyton, grabbing her tight and holding onto her for dear life. She had never been so happy to see her child.

"Mommy, what's wrong? Why are you crying?" Peyton asked.

"I told y'all she was fine." Aunt Connie walked into the foyer, shaking her head, followed by Jordan.

"Girl, your mother and father have been worried sick," Janelle told her. "Where have you been?"

"I had a meeting after school for SAT prep," Peyton said when Sylvia finally let her go.

"You're lying." Sylvia's joy now turned to anger. "I went to the office when you weren't outside, and they said there were no after-school activities."

Peyton looked from her mother to her father to both her aunts. "It wasn't at school. It was at the Campbell Community Center."

Sylvia noticed the slight frown on Jordan's face when Peyton gave her explanation.

"Why didn't you let someone know? Why didn't you respond to any of our calls or texts?" Garry asked.

"I sent Mom a text before my phone died. I told her where I was going, and I already had a ride home," Peyton explained.

"I didn't get a text from you, Peyton," Sylvia snapped, wondering why Peyton was trying to play her for a fool.

"I sent it, I swear," Peyton whined. "I don't know why you didn't get it."

Sylvia reached onto the table near the door and grabbed her cell phone, which was lying there. She opened up her messages and showed Peyton the log, proving that there was no message about an SAT prep course.

"How did you get home?" Sylvia asked. Campbell Community Center was across town and too far for Peyton to walk. No public transportation ran near their neighborhood.

"Coach Dragas was there, and she gave me a ride."

Coach Dragas was Peyton's volleyball and track coach and had given her plenty of rides before, but normally she came inside and talked when she dropped Peyton off.

"Well, I have a birthday dinner to get to," Janelle said, excusing herself.

In the excitement of everything that was going on, Sylvia momentarily forgot that it was her sister's birthday.

"Oh, hell, my bad. Happy birthday." Sylvia hugged her.

"Happy birthday, sis." Garry smiled and hugged her as well.

"Happy birthday, Auntie!" It was Peyton's turn to hug Janelle. "Are we still having your birthday breakfast in the morning?" They had planned to meet the next day to celebrate as a family, followed by mani/pedis at the nail spa.

"Ummmm, now you know Auntie is partying tonight, so we will be having brunch. I will see you all at about eleven, right?" Janelle asked.

"After the stunt you just pulled, you may not be going anywhere, young lady," Garry said. "You're on punishment."

"What stunt?" Peyton cried. "I explained where I was."

"And that's my cue to leave. I will see y'all tomorrow." Janelle eased out the door.

"Daddy, why am I being punished?" Peyton cried out again.

"Peyton, you've been gone for three hours and no one knew where you were," Sylvia said.

"From what I hear, she was gone longer than that, and she didn't get punished." Peyton looked over at her mother.

"What are you tryna say?" Jordan snapped.

"I ain't *tryna* say nothing!" Peyton's voice went up an octave. "I think I said it very clear."

"My taking a walk has nothing to do with your little disappearing act. Don't try to bring me into this, because you definitely don't want it, boo!" Jordan stepped in front of Peyton.

Tension filled the room, and Aunt Connie quickly grabbed Jordan by the arm. "Come on, Jordan. Let's go take another walk now."

"Yeah, walk away," Peyton said, rolling her eyes.

"Peyton!" Sylvia barked.

"Yes?" Peyton asked when Jordan and Aunt Connie were out of the room.

"What is going on with you?"

"Nothing. I haven't done anything wrong. I tried texting you to let you know where I would be. I don't know why you didn't get it. I am home before dark, and I'm fine. Okay, I came home late from school on a Friday evening. I'm seventeen years old, and you all treat me like I'm twelve, and it's not fair." Peyton was now full-blown crying.

"Baby, listen. We were worried, that's all. We know that you're seventeen and you're growing up, but you've gotta communicate better," Garry said and looked over at Sylvia. "We all do, including myself."

"I'm sorry," Peyton said.

Sylvia stared at the two loves of her life standing side by side. The two of them meant everything to her. So much about their family was changing, and it seemed as if everything was happening at once. Her eyes met Garry's, and she thought about the afternoon they just shared and how he dropped everything to be by her side while they were dealing with the crisis that evening. She knew that as much as she loved her daughter, she trusted her about as much as she trusted her husband right about now.

Janelle

The entire family had enjoyed a wonderful brunch on Saturday morning as part of Janelle's birthday weekend, and the ladies were now heading to the nail spa, minus Garry. As they were leaving the restaurant, Jordan went to get into the car with her father, but Sylvia stopped her.

"Where are you going young lady?" she asked.

Jordan looked confused by the question. "With my father."

"We have plans," Sylvia said.

"Huh?" Jordan looked around, confused.

Janelle walked over and stood beside her sister. "Hello, it's my birthday! Ladies' day out!"

Jordan still looked confused, so Janelle grabbed her by the hand and said, "Tell your daddy goodbye and let's go."

"I don't think—" Jordan started.

"You don't have to think," Sylvia said. "You're a child. We think for you."

"Have fun, ladies." Garry waved.

"Trust me. We're all going shopping with your credit card. We will," Janelle yelled to him and laughed. She then put her arms around the young girl's shoulders and said, "Now, come on, Jordan."

"Thank you," he mouthed, and she nodded. She somehow got the vibe that the young girl felt like an outsider, and she wanted to make her feel like a part of the family. She even let Jordan pick out what color she should get for her nails and toes.

"Oh, my goodness, I needed this," Janelle moaned as the technician massaged her foot. "Ohhhhh, yessss!"

"Do you really have to sound like that?" Sylvia asked.

"You shoulda heard how I sounded last night." Janelle winked.

"Grossss!" Sylvia responded with a look of devastation on her face.

"I hope you made sure he wrapped it up if he was making you sound like that," Aunt Connie told her.

"Aunt Connie!" Sylvia gasped. "There are children here."

Janelle leaned up and looked over at Aunt Connie, who was seated between Peyton and Jordan. Both girls were laughing.

"What children?" Aunt Connie said. "They are both young women, and they both know about wrapping it up, don't you? I already schooled them. They will not be included in the statistics of newly contracted HIV or pregnant teens."

"Please stop, Aunt Connie," Janelle pleaded. "It's my birthday."

"I just want to remind you in case you decide to have birthday sex: wrap it up." Aunt Connie nodded. The tiny older woman seated on the stool in front of her aunt, rubbing her feet, looked up and nodded. "See, even she knows."

"Where did you go last night?" Sylvia asked.

Janelle was grateful that her sister was making an effort to change the subject.

"Went to dinner at Malibu's. That new Jamaican spot," Janelle answered, her eyes still closed as she continued to enjoy her foot massage.

"How was it?"

"The food was good, the service was slow, and the crowd was okay." Janelle shrugged.

"You don't sound too excited. What happened?"

"Nivea happened." Janelle frowned.

For the most part, she had enjoyed having dinner with her friends. It was completed with her being serenaded with a reggae version of "Happy Birthday" by the staff and the band, and then a cake from her favorite bakery. But Nivea and her behavior had cut their evening and their plans short. She was used to her best friend getting tipsy and being loud, but for some reason it seemed extra boisterous last night. She kept asking about where Jarvis was and what he had planned for Janelle's birthday.

"He was all over you last night. Y'all look so good together!" Nivea leaned over and pushed her shoulder. "That man is in love with you."

"Nivea, what the hell are you talking about?" Natalie laughed. "You are drunk."

"Now is neither the time nor place," Janelle said, looking around the table. Although everyone there was someone Janelle considered a friend, her relationship status with Jarvis was not something she wanted to discuss in front of them.

"I'm trying to help you," Nivea said.

"It's not that serious, Niv." Janelle shook her head. Her phone vibrated, and she saw that it was a text from Titus.

Hey, baby.

Hey, T. *She texted back.*

I have something for you, *he told her.*

Really what? *she asked.*

He responded with a picture of himself, holding a chocolate cupcake with one single lit candle.

Janelle smiled and sent him a thank you text with a kissy face.

Love you, *his last text read, and she put her phone on the table beside her.*

"Are you listening to me?" Nivea's voice got louder.

"Sorry. I'm listening," Janelle told her.

"This thing between you and Jarvis, it is serious! You just don't see it. You know what your problem is?" Nivea frowned.

"I don't have a problem." Janelle forced herself to act amused, although she wasn't.

"Yes, you do." Nivea reached across and grabbed Janelle's phone. She moved her fingers across the screen and then held it up, showing a picture of Titus, who had sent another message. "This is your problem. You can't see what you have with Jarvis because of this. This isn't real."

"Give me that." Janelle snatched the phone from her.

"You are going to lose a good man if you don't start acting like you want him."

"Where is this coming from?" Janelle looked over at Natalie.

"I don't know." Natalie shrugged. "Probably all those rum punches she's been sucking down."

"I just want my best friend to be happy! I want us all to fall in love and be happy! It's your birthday!" Nivea screamed, leaning over to hug Janelle but knocking their drinks over in the process.

She was now not only embarrassed but pissed at her friend's behavior.

"That's it. It's time to go," Janelle said, standing up from the table. "Come on, Niv. Let's get you home."

"Nooooo, we're supposed to go to the club! It's still early!" Nivea whined.

She was right. It wasn't even ten o'clock. It was still early, but Nivea was in no condition to go to the club or anywhere else. Janelle couldn't believe she had gotten drunk so quickly.

"I'll drive her, Nellie," Natalie said, looking disappointed. "You guys can go ahead and enjoy the remainder of your evening."

"No, I'll take her," Janelle said. They paid the tab, thanked the other guests, and led Nivea out the door.

"Where did you park?" Natalie asked Nivea, reaching into her sister's purse for her keys.

Nivea looked around the parking lot and laughed. "I don't remember."

"Forget it," Natalie said.

They decided that Natalie would just take Nivea to her house, and she would bring her back the following day to get her car from the restaurant parking lot.

"Leave it to Nivea." Sylvia laughed after Janelle told her what had happened. "Always the life of the party."

"Yeah, I guess." Janelle sat back and closed her eyes.

"Have you talked to her today?" Sylvia asked.

"Nope," Janelle said, and she didn't plan on speaking with her either. It wasn't that she was mad or upset, but she knew that if she had spoken with Nivea, her friend would be ready to continue the partying, which had gotten cut short. Besides, Janelle already had plans for the evening; plans that she really didn't wish to explain to her best friend. At least, not yet.

It was nearly seven o'clock, and Janelle had changed outfits four times. Clothes were strewn all over her bedroom, and her quest for the perfect ensemble for her dinner date seemed to be impossible. She had gone from a casual pair of fitted jeans that showed off her butt perfectly, along with her favorite top, which happened to have a plunging neckline, to a sleek, form-fitting black dress that hugged her curves and showed off her shapely calves. Any other time, she would have called Nivea, who had the ability to pick out the perfect fly outfit no matter the occasion. Making that call was definitely not an option. She settled on the jeans with a simple, ivory off-the-shoulder blouse and a pair of red heels: casual, chic, and sexy. She put the finishing touches on her hair, jewelry, and makeup. She checked her reflection in the mirror to make sure she looked fierce, but not overdone.

"Definitely not bad for thirty-eight," she said to herself. She grabbed the red Michael Kors purse Sylvia had just given her for her birthday and headed downstairs to wait for Sherrod's arrival. For some reason, her stomach was quivering. She went into the kitchen to pour herself a glass of wine when she heard the doorbell.

"Happy birthday," Sherrod said, holding a gift bag and another small box. Dressed in jeans, a white dress shirt, a sports jacket, and black shoes, he looked amazing.

"Thank you." Janelle smiled, greeting him with a hug and holding the door for him to come inside.

"These are for you." He handed her the items he was holding.

"Awww, thank you!" Janelle said. They went into the living room, and she put them on the table. "You look nice."

"And you look gorgeous. You can open your gifts before we go."

Janelle reached for the greeting card, which was taped to a box, and opened it. It was a corny, comical card, and it made her laugh. She opened the box, and inside was a beautiful hand-painted wine glass with her name in red.

"It's beautiful, Sherrod. How did you know red is my favorite color?" she asked.

"Well, the fact that you're a Delta was my first clue." He laughed, pointing to the sorority paraphernalia in the corner. "Your car is red, your workout sneakers are red, so I figured you have a thing for the color."

"You are right," she told him, admiring the glass.

"Open the bag," he said.

She reached inside the red gift bag and pulled out a bottle of Chardonnay. She read the label, which she could barely pronounce.

"It's French," he explained. "I visited a vineyard in one of the provinces when I was in France about a year ago, and I fell in love with it. I saw you had a bottle of Chardonnay in your fridge the other night, so I thought you might like it."

Janelle stood and listened to him in disbelief. "You visited a vineyard in France?"

Sherrod laughed. "Yes, in France. I plan on going to a couple of Australian vineyards this summer."

"Wow." Janelle stared at the bottle, which was almost as beautiful as the glass he had given her.

"We'd better get going. I made reservations for dinner. Are you ready?"

Janelle was still trying to comprehend the fact that he had traveled to France and planned on going to Australia in a few months. Traveling the world and exploring international places was something she loved.

"Yeah, let me grab a jacket," she told him. She went to the hall closet and grabbed her blazer.

Twenty minutes later, they pulled in front of what looked like a small cottage nestled in the downtown area of the city. She looked around, trying to figure out exactly where they were. The small wooden sign outside read: MUEHLERS.

"Have you ever been here?" Sherrod asked.

"I don't even know where we are," Janelle said.

"Good," Sherrod said, hopping out and rushing to open her car door. She stepped outside, and they went to the door, where a maître d' greeted them.

"Welcome to Muehler's."

Once inside, Janelle was taken aback by the beauty of what she now realized was a wine bistro. It was quaint, cozy, filled with the sound of jazz and the smell of great food. Sherrod gave them his name, and they were led to their table.

"How did you find this place?" Janelle asked after she was seated.

"Someone told me about it."

The waiter came over and explained the specials and the featured wines of the evening. They were just about to order when a short, balding man walked over and greeted them.

"Rod, how are you, sir? I'm so glad you came in tonight. Is everything okay?"

"Walter, my man." Sherrod stood up and shook the man's hand. "Everything is great. We just got here. This is my friend, Janelle Hayes."

"Ms. Hayes, pleased to meet you. Please enjoy yourselves, and if you need anything, just let me know. My staff knows to make sure you are well taken care of, Rod," Walter told them.

"Thanks, Walter," Sherrod said.

"Who is that?" Janelle asked.

"That's Walter Muehler. He owns the place."

"How do you know the owner? Wait, Walter Muehler? *The* Walter Muehler? As in the Muehler Foundation?" Janelle asked, referring to the family that, in their city, was equivalent to the Rockefellers and probably had just as much money.

"Yep," Sherrod said casually.

"How do you know Walter Muehler?"

"I'm his friendly neighborhood pharmacist. He comes into the store all the time."

"Un-freaking-believable." Janelle shook her head and laughed.

The two of them enjoyed a great meal and shared a bottle of the most amazing wine she had ever tasted. Mr.

Muehler insisted that they both take a bottle home before they left. Sherrod held her hand as they walked to the car.

He opened the door and asked, "Did you have a nice time?"

"I had a wonderful time." Janelle smiled at him. It had to be one of the best dates she had ever been on. Sherrod was funny, entertaining, and fascinating, and she was glad she had decided to go to dinner, birthday or not.

"I'm glad, because I am having a wonderful time too. Happy birthday." He leaned over and kissed her softly on the cheek. It was quick, gentle, and unexpected; but for Janelle, it was nice. She climbed into his car with a smile.

"So, you are really into wine, huh?" Janelle said as they drove out of the parking lot.

"I guess you could say that." Sherrod laughed. "It wasn't something I planned as a hobby. My best friend was a master sommelier, and I sort of got hooked on tastings and visiting vineyards."

"My best friend is somewhat of a sommelier too." Janelle laughed. Then she quickly realized he knew who her best friend was and regretted saying it.

"Yeah, Nivea can toss them back. She always could, but that's what makes her Nivea." Sherrod nodded.

"I can imagine how she was back in middle school."

"The same as she is now: beautiful, loud, smart, and she could always dress her tail off. She was best dressed girl in middle school and high school."

Janelle listened to him talk about memories of how Nivea would cheer him on from the sidelines while he ran track and field, and how no one expected a nerd like him to be dating a firecracker like Nivea.

"We were like night and day, but she was so cool. I couldn't believe that day at her house when she told me she wanted me to be the one. I was nervous as hell because I knew if anything went wrong, she was gonna tell everybody." Sherrod laughed.

"The one what?" Janelle asked.

"Wait, Nivea didn't tell you?" he said with a cautious look.

"She told me she's known you since middle school and you were friends."

"Oh, damn. I thought you knew." Sherrod sat back in his seat. He paused a moment, then said. "Janelle, I was Nivea's first."

"First what?" Janelle's heart began pounding, and she prayed he wasn't about to say what she thought he was.

"I was the guy she lost her virginity to."

Janelle's jaw dropped. She felt nauseous and closed her eyes. Just as she was about to ask Sherrod why he hadn't said something earlier, her cell phone rang. Taking it out of her purse and seeing it was Peyton, Janelle prayed that nothing was wrong.

She answered, "What's wrong, P?"

"Hey, Aunt Nellie. Nothing's wrong. I need to ask you a favor."

"What is it? I'm kind of busy right now."

"Are you on a date?" Peyton asked.

"Yes. Now, what do you want?" Janelle glanced over at Sherrod, who was happily humming along to some ridiculous rap song on the radio and acting as if what he'd just said moments before wasn't a big deal at all.

"I need to know if I can spend the night at your house next weekend. Please say yes!" Peyton pleaded.

"Why?" Janelle asked.

"I need a break from here, and I will explain it to you. But I'm begging you. It's important."

"We'll see. I'll call you tomorrow," Janelle told her. Now that she knew it wasn't an emergency, she wanted to cut their conversation short and get back to Sherrod.

"Wait," Peyton said.

"What?" Janelle whispered. "I'm on a date, remember."

"I know, and I'm sorry. But I'm gonna need for you to act like this is your idea and ask my mom," Peyton told her.

Janelle knew her niece was up to something. "We'll talk tomorrow."

"Thanks, Aunt Nellie."

"I didn't say yes. I gotta go," Janelle said.

"Wait, one more thing!" Peyton yelled.

"What? Hurry up," Janelle hissed into the phone.

"Remember what Aunt Connie said. Be safe and make sure he wraps it up!"

Janelle hung the phone up without responding to her niece. They pulled into her driveway, and Sherrod turned the car off. When they were finishing up their meal, she had invited him back to her place for a glass of wine. Now, she wasn't so sure that was a good idea.

"Are you all right?" he asked.

"I'm fine," she told him, looking over at him. He was staring at her and smiling, and she asked. "What?"

"I'm not getting you into any kind of trouble, am I?"

"Trouble? With who?" she asked, confused by his question.

"Your boo," he responded.

"I told you I don't have a boo. Jarvis is just my friend." Janelle shook her head, thinking he had a nerve referring to Jarvis when he had just confessed that he'd deflowered her best friend.

"I wasn't talking about Jarvis."

"Then who are you talking about?" Janelle looked at him.

"Your other boo, the married one from the gym."

Janelle's mouth opened, but nothing came out. Sherrod got out, opened her door, and she stared at him. For the second time that night, he had rendered her speechless:

first, when he told her about being Nivea's first, and now asking about Titus.

"That's not my boo either," Janelle finally said.

"Let me guess. That's your friend too."

"I'm not saying anything." She shook her head. It was the first time another guy had ever asked her about Titus, and she didn't know how to explain it.

Sherrod said, "Good. I wouldn't believe you anyway."

Sylvia

"I need to talk," Janelle said. It was eight thirty on a Sunday morning, so Sylvia knew whatever it was had to be important. Her sister never liked getting up early.

"What's wrong?" Sylvia asked.

"Can you please meet me at Starbucks?"

"I'm getting ready for church, Janelle. You should be too, as a matter of fact."

"Can you meet me afterwards?" Janelle asked.

"Just come over to the house."

"No, I can't deal with Aunt Connie. Not today. I don't have the energy or the patience."

"Fine," Sylvia said. She agreed to meet her sister in an hour at the Starbucks closest to the church.

"What's wrong?" Garry rolled over and asked. He reached out and touched her thigh.

How he had ended up in their bed, she didn't know, because she definitely didn't tell him he could sleep there. However, she didn't complain when she felt him climb beside her and put his arms around her body either.

"Janelle is having some sort of crisis. I am gonna go meet her." She exhaled as she sat up.

"I thought we agreed we would be going to church today as a family," Garry reminded her.

"We are. I will make sure everyone is up before I leave, and I can just meet you all there," Sylvia told him. She hoped he was wise enough to realize that he was still not out of the dog house yet, and she was not gonna deal with his demanding nature. It was too soon. She told him, "We are still going to church as a family, just in two separate cars."

"Is Aunt Connie going with you?" Garry asked.

"No, she's not. Bring her with you."

Sylvia got out of the bed and headed into the bathroom. She heard Garry groaning and couldn't help giggling. The thought of Garry in the car with Aunt Connie and the girls was too funny, and she could only imagine the conversation they would be having.

When she arrived at Starbucks an hour later, Janelle was sitting at a table dressed in a sweat suit and a pair of sunglasses, picking at a chocolate croissant. Sylvia ordered a grande latte, something she could have had every day if Aunt Connie would let her use the Keurig.

"Rough night?" Sylvia asked as she sat across from her sister.

"That's an understatement." Janelle took her shades off.

"Well, you don't look that hung over, so it couldn't be that bad."

"You're not going to believe this." Janelle sighed. "Last night, I went on the best date of my life."

"With Jarvis?" Sylvia smiled.

"No."

"Please don't tell me you went on a date with Titus. If that's what you brought me here to talk about, I'm leaving." Sylvia reached for her purse, preparing to leave.

"No, not with him. I went with Sherrod."

"Who is Sherrod?" Sylvia was confused. She knew Janelle had been dating Jarvis for the past few months and never heard her talk about anyone else.

Sylvia listened to her sister talk about the man she had recently met. He happened to not only be a handsome, caring pharmacist, but also the man who had taken her best friend's virginity.

"Damn! I take it Nivea doesn't know you went out with him?" Sylvia raised an eyebrow.

"No, she doesn't know." Janelle looked at Sylvia like she was crazy.

"Are you gonna tell her?"

"I can't. I think she likes him."

"If you think she likes him, why did you go out with him? What is wrong with you?" Sylvia stared and waited for Janelle's answer.

"I went out with him because he took care of me while I was sick, and it was my birthday, and he asked me out. It was the least I could do. I thought we were going out as friends."

"You know, Janelle, you and this term you keep casually using: *friends*? You really need to look it up in the dictionary. According to you, Titus is your friend, and so is Jarvis. Speaking of Jarvis, does he know about your date with your *friend* Sherrod?" Sylvia shook her head.

"No, he doesn't. And even if he did, there was nothing there. He is the last person who should have anything to say. He is the one who said we are keeping it casual and free to see other people. I'm not worried about Jarvis," Janelle replied.

"You were worried about him when you saw him out with his coworker the other week," Sylvia reminded her.

"You are not helping me figure this out, Syl. What am I gonna do?"

Her sister seemed to really be in a state of confusion, and she wondered if there was something more that she wasn't telling. She decided to ask her the burning question. "Did you sleep with Sherrod last night?"

"What? No!" Janelle snapped.

"Don't get all defensive. That was a valid question." Sylvia took a sip of her latte.

"No, I didn't sleep with him. I swear."

"Did you do anything with him?" Sylvia stared. "I know you, Janelle. I am sure you didn't go back to your place and play Uno for the rest of the night. What did y'all do?"

"We drank the bottle of wine he gave me for my birthday," Janelle said.

"And?"

"And we talked."

"And?"

"And he kissed me," Janelle admitted. "But it was on the cheek."

"And?"

"And it was nice."

"Don't play with me, Janelle."

"Fine, there was some touching. While we were talking, he gave me a foot rub."

From the way she answered, Sylvia knew Janelle was telling the truth. She also knew that whoever this Sherrod guy was, Janelle like him. A lot.

"You have to talk to Nivea and tell her."

"I can't. She's gonna be pissed. And nothing major happened. I swear," Janelle said, "But she's still gonna be mad."

"You should have told her before last night. You should have told her when he brought the medicine to your house," Sylvia pointed out.

"Why? I didn't go after him behind her back," Janelle told her.

"But you knew you were attracted to him, and he was attracted to you. And out of respect for the friendship that you all have, you should've just been honest and up front. You took the coward's way out because you wanted to avoid confrontation."

"She's gonna be pissed."

"And hurt. But it's better that you come clean and tell her now before she finds out sixteen years from now that you and Sherrod have a fifteen-year-old daughter that she never knew about." Sylvia sipped her coffee, which was now getting cold.

"This is not the same thing." Janelle shook her head.

"It is. A lie is a lie. You're already involved in one situation revolving around a lie, but I'm not gonna go there. Don't make this a habit or a pattern. Be a grown woman and own your decisions. You met a nice guy and there was some chemistry. It happens all the time. She's your best friend. She deserves to be told. From what you've told me, it seems that this Sherrod guy is feeling you just as much as you're feeling him. Talk to her together."

"Maybe that will be better." Janelle nodded.

"If it's any consolation, I'm glad you met someone who you seem to actually like for a change. Don't get me wrong; I know you like Jarvis and he is a great guy, but I know you're settling when it comes to him. From how you're acting right now, you actually seem to be smitten with this Sherrod guy, and I'm happy for you. I hope you actually open yourself to the possibility of what may be love. You deserve to know what real love feels like."

"I know what real love feels like." Janelle laughed.

"Fine, what real love feels like and not with someone who's unavailable because they're already married or a commitment phobe." Sylvia looked down at her watch and saw that it was time for her to go. She stood up and gave Janelle a hug. "I gotta go. You know I love you."

"I love you too. Thank you."

"You're welcome. Talk to Nivea and call me later."

"Oh, Syl," Janelle said. "Can I get Peyton next weekend?"

"For what?"

"Some PJ Time," Janelle said. "We haven't had any in a while. I had fun hanging out with her yesterday."

From the time Peyton could walk, her sister would always have what they affectionately called "PJ Time," which was slumber parties in their pajamas just for Janelle and Peyton. It had been a while since they'd had one.

"You know she's on punishment."

"Not from me," Janelle said. "Don't even try it. Besides, I'm gonna need someone to eat ice cream with and watch chick flicks, because after I talk to Nivea, I won't have a best friend."

"Fine." Sylvia gave in. She tossed her cup in the trash and headed to meet her family for worship.

Church service seemed to be exactly what Sylvia needed. It was as if the pastor were speaking directly to her and Garry as he preached on grace and forgiveness. Throughout his message, Aunt Connie, who happened to be seated to her left, kept nudging her and nodding her head in agreement so much that her neck had to be sore.

It had been a while since Sylvia had been to church, and she knew people had been talking about Garry's "new daughter" who now lived with them; however, no one said anything out of the ordinary to any of them. Everyone acted like having Jordan there with them was as normal as the choir singing during offering time.

"Where is Jordan?" Sylvia asked Peyton when it was time to leave. The two girls had attended youth service, which was held in another part of the church, and they were supposed to meet in the vestibule of the building.

"I don't know." Peyton shrugged. She was there waiting by the door, but there was no sign of Jordan anywhere.

"What do you mean, *you don't know*?" Garry grumbled. "Weren't you together in youth church?"

"I was, then she left out. I saw her a little while ago talking to some dude," Peyton told them.

"What dude? Where?" Garry's voice escalated, and Sylvia touched his arm to calm him down because there were people now looking.

"Garry, I'll go look for her," Sylvia told him. "We'll meet you at the car."

"No, I'll go look for her. Where did you see her?" Garry turned to Peyton.

"On the back side of the building in the hallway," Peyton told him.

Garry grabbed her by the arm and said, "Come and show me where!"

"Ouch!" Peyton exclaimed as he pulled her along.

"Garry, you're hurting her," Sylvia told him. "Let her go."

Garry wasn't listening. He continued holding onto Peyton, and they went down the corridor of the church toward the back of the building. Sylvia's heart began pounding as she rushed behind them. She was relieved that before they could get much farther, she saw Jordan heading toward them.

"Where were you?" he barked.

"I went to the bathroom." Jordan looked at all of them like they were crazy. "It was crowded in there."

"What man were you talking to?" Garry asked her.

"What are you talking about?" Jordan's eyes widened, and her body stiffened.

"I know you were in the back hallway talking to a man! Who was it?"

Sylvia watched as Jordan's eyes glanced at Peyton, who was standing beside her father.

"I don't know what you're talking about. The only person I was talking to was the usher who showed me where the bathroom was."

"Lord, I been looking all over for y'all," Aunt Connie walked up and told them.

"You're lying," Garry said to Jordan. "Let me find out he—"

"Find out what? And why do I have to lie? I went to the bathroom, and if someone said anything different, then maybe they are the ones lying! Instead of accusing me of doing something, maybe you should be worried about who was all hugged up and kissing in the church parking lot when they were supposed to be in youth service!" Jordan snapped.

Garry's attention turned to Peyton, who now looked shocked.

"What is she talking about, Peyton?"

"She's lying," Peyton fired back.

Jordan looked at Peyton and said icily, "I don't have to lie, but apparently you do."

"I wasn't kissing anyone," Peyton cried.

"I don't want to talk about it anymore. Let's just leave." Garry walked away without saying another word. Sylvia stared at both girls and directed them toward the door.

"Mom —" Peyton said.

"I don't want to hear another word, Peyton Janelle." Sylvia glared at her.

Garry decided he needed some alone time, so everyone rode in the car with Sylvia. Aunt Connie tried making small talk, but even her going on and on about what she planned on making for the upcoming bake sale wasn't enough to cut the tension. Just when Sylvia thought things were getting better with her marriage, it seemed that things between Jordan and Peyton were getting worse, and she didn't know what to do.

Janelle

"Damn, I've been trying to reach you all weekend," Titus said. "How was your birthday?"

"It was great," Janelle told him. "Hung out with my girls and my family."

"Did you get my gift?" he asked her.

She was sitting in her car in the parking lot of the gym and was just about to go in when he had called her.

"What gift?" she asked him.

"Your cupcake." He laughed. "It was chocolate, your favorite."

"Yes, I got it." She sighed.

"What's wrong, Nellie?"

"Nothing. I just got a lot on my mind, I guess."

"I really was hoping I could see you for your birthday, but Tarik had a semi-final game Saturday night, and I was caught up in that," Titus told her. "You know how that goes."

"I understand."

"I'm glad you had a good time though, baby. Did Jamaal take you out?"

"His name is Jarvis, and no, we actually didn't even go out this weekend," Janelle told him. Jarvis had called her Sunday night asking her out, but she declined his offer. She was starting to realize that she was no longer a priority for him, which was apparent from his last-minute invites. She wasn't upset or even disappointed.

"Really? That's crazy. I thought things were going well for you guys. But if he didn't take you out for your birthday, I know he's no longer competition." Titus laughed. "So, did y'all break up or something?"

"We weren't really together," Janelle answered. "We were just dating, that's all."

Suddenly, she looked up and saw Sherrod walking into the gym.

"Hey, look, I gotta call you back." Janelle got out of her car, grabbed her gym bag, and went inside. She had thought about Sylvia's suggestion about talking to Sherrod and telling Nivea together.

After changing her clothes, she walked into the workout area and found him on one of the elliptical machines. Instead of walking over to him, she decided to send him a simple text that said, I see you, to his phone. She then climbed onto her usual treadmill, hit the playlist on her iPhone, and got to work.

Twenty minutes later, she saw him smiling at his phone and looking for her. She pretended to be focused on running until he walked over and stood in front of her machine. She took out her ear buds.

"What's up?" He grinned.

"Nothing much," Janelle huffed, still maintaining her stride on the machine. "How are you?"

"I'm good. You almost done here?"

"I can be," she told him and slowed down to a walk before stopping completely. She hadn't done a full thirty-minute run as she planned, but talking with Sherrod was worth cutting her time short.

"Wanna grab a smoothie?" he asked her.

"Sure."

They went over to the juice bar and ordered.

"How was the rest of your birthday weekend?"

"It was pretty uneventful. I managed to get some rest before going back to work today. Luckily, I did have my doctor's note, because I know my boss thought I was faking since it was my birthday week," she said, sipping her smoothie.

"Yeah, I probably woulda thought the same thing," he told her.

Janelle continued to make small talk as she tried to think of a way to bring up her concerns about Nivea finding out about them dating. She didn't want to make the assumption there would be a second date, especially when he hadn't even brought up seeing her again.

"I really want to thank you again for all you did last week and Saturday night. I had a great time."

"Me too. I was wondering, if you're not busy this Saturday—" Sherrod's phone began vibrating, and he looked at it. "I gotta take this. Excuse me."

Janelle sat back, smiling. He was about to ask her on a second date. But, as much as that thought excited her, she knew that she definitely had to tell Nivea.

"Hey, sweetheart, what's going on?" she heard him say into the phone. At the word *sweetheart*, she couldn't help but listen closer. "I don't know about that. I know you do. I know it's important. I know. Yes. Are you sure? Sweetie, you know I understand. Yes. Fine, I will see you Saturday."

Sherrod came back over and sat down. He looked worried.

"Is everything okay?" she asked him.

"Yeah, everything's cool," he told her. "Listen, I'm sorry. I got some errands to run. I will talk to you later."

Sherrod got up and walked away, leaving Janelle sitting at the table alone. She was stunned for a minute, and then she was glad she hadn't mentioned anything to Nivea, because based on what had just happened, there wouldn't be another date for her to worry about.

"Is this seat taken?"

Janelle looked up to see Titus standing in front of her, holding a chocolate cupcake, her favorite.

"Aunt Nelle!" Peyton screamed as she ran down the steps, carrying a laptop bag in one hand and a small suitcase in the other.

"Peyton!" Janelle mocked her niece's voice.

"Let's go!" Peyton told her.

"Lord, child, I just walked in the door. Can I at least speak to my sister and my aunt?" Janelle said. "Where are they?"

"Mommy's not here, and Aunt Connie is in the den watching *Law and Order*, as usual," Peyton said.

Janelle walked into the den and spoke to her aunt. "Hey, Aunt Connie."

"Hey, Janelle. How you feeling?" Aunt Connie got up and gave her a hug.

"I'm fine. How are you?"

"I'm good. You here to pick up Peyton? Y'all ain't have to invite me to your li'l slumber party. I didn't wanna come anyway," Aunt Connie teased.

"You know you don't need an invitation, Aunt Connie. You are always welcome to come and hang out. Go pack a bag and let's roll," Janelle told her.

"No!" Peyton said quickly. "This is a PJ party. No one else allowed! Come on, Aunt Nellie. Let's go!"

"All right, Aunt Connie. We are gone. Tell Sylvia I'll call her later."

"You girls be careful," Aunt Connie told them

"We will," Peyton said, dragging Janelle with her.

They were about to walk out the door when Jordan walked out of the kitchen.

"Hey, Jordan." Janelle smiled.

"Hey."

"What's up?" Janelle asked, thinking that maybe she should have suggested Peyton include her in their weekend plans.

"Nothing much. Have fun," she said and walked past them hurriedly.

Janelle looked over at Peyton, who shrugged and rushed out the door.

"Okay, what's this about?" she asked her niece when they finally got in the car. "What's his name?"

"Who?" Peyton asked innocently.

"Whoever has you scheming like this. Tell me."

"Promise me you won't say anything, Aunt Nellie," Peyton pleaded.

"I promise."

"His name is Tank. He's tall, funny, smart, and he is just amazing," Peyton gushed. "And he's talented and caring, and he's just different."

"He sounds great. Does he go to your school?"

"No, he goes to a different high school. I barely get to see him. But we talk, text, and Skype every day, and he makes me feel . . . I can't describe it, Aunt Nellie."

Janelle noticed the look on her niece's face that she knew too well. It was the look of happiness, contentment, and sheer joy. Peyton was in love.

"Well, he sounds great. What does that have to do with this weekend?"

"He plays basketball, and tonight is the state championship game. I need for you to take me to go see him play. It's in Madison."

"Madison? What? Are you crazy? That's like five hours away, Peyton."

"I know, and the game starts at seven tonight, so we need to be leaving now." Peyton pointed at the dashboard clock of Janelle's car.

"Is this the boy you were kissing at church that your mom was telling me about?" Janelle asked.

Peyton didn't have to answer. The look on her face told it all. "It wasn't a kiss like that. He came to church to see me. To church. Doesn't that say something about how nice of a guy he is?"

"Then why can't you introduce him to your mom and dad, Peyton? Why can't you be honest and tell them what's going on?"

"Because they aren't trying to hear it." Peyton shook her head. "I have no freedom, and they aren't trying to give me any. And, Aunt Nelle, you know I haven't given them any reason *not* to trust me. I make good grades, keep my room clean; I do whatever they ask of me. I am a good person." Tears began to well up in Peyton's eyes.

"I know you are, baby, and I am so proud of the young woman that you are becoming. You have made some good decisions in life—some great ones, as a matter of fact. But this one, this sneaking around and hiding it, it's not right. Your parents love you. We all do. And it's clear that you love this guy."

"I do love him." Peyton nodded. "And he loves me too. He tells me every day."

Janelle's mind flashed back to Saturday night, when she and Sherrod were sitting on her sofa, enjoying her birthday wine. They were talking about dating and relationships and how difficult it was to find love.

Sherrod had said, "See, the problem is that some of us are holding on to people who says that they love us but are still not willing to publicly announce it. But don't you want to be with someone who loves you enough that they don't care if the whole world knows it? I blame technology. Instead of real relationships, we got these *e-lationships* that consist of emails, texts, inboxes and phone calls, but no real intimacy. I personally want something real, and I'm not settling for anything less."

When he'd said it, as he stared at her and rubbed her feet, Janelle felt a connection she had only felt with one other person, and in that moment, she panicked. Now, as she listened to her niece talk about her new love, whom she communicated with daily via the phone or computer, Janelle knew what Sherrod meant.

"Peyton, if he loves you, then he will have no problem meeting your family. He should care enough about you to want to meet them. You are smart, beautiful, and talented. You have an amazing future ahead of you, and most of all, you're respectful. Any man who deserves you will want to preserve that. Not only should he want to meet your family, but he should introduce you to his family too. You're too good to be sneaking around, and you're too wonderful to be kept as someone's secret," Janelle told her. "Don't you see that?"

"Yes." Peyton nodded. "I get it."

"Now, I promised you something, so I need for you to promise me something."

"Okay, what?"

"Promise me that any guy that you date, you will invite him over and introduce him to your mom and dad. Not just him, but any guy you develop serious feelings for," Janelle said.

"I will." Peyton smiled.

"And this basketball game will be the last event that you sneak to." Janelle shook her head.

Peyton looked over at her and squealed. "Auntie, we can go? Really?"

"I guess our PJ party has turned into a PJ road trip." Janelle pulled her sunglasses over her eyes and cranked up the radio. They had a long ride ahead of them.

The convention center where the state basketball championship was being played was packed with people.

Janelle and Peyton maneuvered their way up the bleachers and found two great seats near center court. The ride wasn't as bad as Janelle thought it would be, but she'd had enough sense to stop and grab a change of clothes in case she didn't feel like driving back home afterward. Seeing all the people that had gathered, she hoped they would be able to find a hotel room nearby if they decided to stay.

"Oh, my goodness, look at all these people," Peyton said. "This is crazy!"

"Yeah, it is."

"Thank you, thank you, thank you." Peyton hugged Janelle's arm tight.

"Yeah, yeah, yeah," Janelle told her. "Thank me by buying me a box of that popcorn that guy is selling."

"No problem!" Peyton said, standing and yelling for the vendor's attention. She bought them each a box of popcorn and a soda.

Just as they started eating, the lights dimmed, and the band began playing a fight song. Janelle looked on the floor, and a group of cheerleaders dressed in white uniforms with orange-and-green trim held up a huge piece of white paper across a doorway. Written on the paper were the words *Go Rattlers*. Seconds later, a group of the tallest boys Janelle had ever seen came bursting through and onto the court.

"Here they come!" Peyton gasped.

"Tank! Tank!" girls cheered all over.

Janelle couldn't help but notice Peyton was not enjoying her boyfriend's supporters.

"Which one is he?" she asked.

Peyton pointed and said, "Number forty-two!"

"He's *cute!*" Janelle said, looking at the tall, baby-face boy who was dribbling the ball between his legs. "Tank! Go, Tank!"

"Oh my God, Aunt Nellie. What are you doing?"

"Didn't we say he should love you enough to let the world know? We drove five hours to see this dude. Trust, he will know you're here. Tank!"

The boy looked up at them, and Janelle waved, pointing to Peyton. A grin spread across his face, and he blew her a kiss and gave her thumbs up. Peyton blew him a kiss back and waved. She looked around at the other random chicks that had been screaming Tank's name and gave them a smug grin.

"See, I told you," Janelle said with a look of satisfaction. "Your Auntie knows these things."

The other team made their entrance, and the two women took their seats.

"Isn't he fine?" Peyton said. "Wait until you see him play. He's a phenomenon. All the schools have been trying to recruit him. And it's not just because of his basketball skills. He's an honors student too."

"That's good," Janelle said between handfuls of popcorn. She noticed the name of the other team and asked, "Drakeville High? Isn't that Jordan's old school?"

"I think so. Wow, I didn't even know that's who they were playing, and she didn't even mention it," Peyton said.

"I'm really gonna need for you to put in a little more effort with her, Peyton. She is your sister," Janelle told her.

"I know, but she's so mean, and she's spoiled. She hardly talks to anyone other than Aunt Connie, which should let you know how crazy she is." Peyton shook her head and sighed.

"Just try." Janelle laughed.

They stood for the singing of the National Anthem, and the announcer began calling the starting lineup for each team. They stood up and screamed along with the remainder of the crowd. Tank was the last player to be called.

"And at forward, standing six foot five inches, number forty-one, Tarik King!"

Janelle felt faint and sat down before her knees buckled beneath her. Of all the boys for her niece to fall in love with, she had to go and fall for Titus's son.

Sylvia

"Those are nice," Lynne said.

Sylvia admired the silver pumps she was trying on in the mirror. She hadn't planned on going shopping, but Lynne called and told her Nordstrom's was having a killer shoe sale, and she couldn't resist.

"They are cute, but where am I gonna wear them?" Sylvia asked. "And what am I gonna wear them with?"

"They would be perfect for your wedding," Lynne told her. "And you'll wear them with your wedding gown."

Sylvia glanced up. "What?"

"Your wedding. The vow renewal. The one that's in like five months. Remember?"

"Girl, I don't even know if we're still doing that." Sylvia sat down and slipped the shoes off, placing them back in the box.

"Why not? You still have time to plan. Not a lot of time, but there's still time."

"It's just not the same. We still have issues, and I just don't know."

"All marriages have issues. Yours is no different. And you're going to therapy to work through those issues, right?"

"Yes, but Garry and I haven't even discussed renewing our vows. We've barely discussed staying married."

"Let's keep it real, Syl. You're going to stay married. You and Garry have more than enough love for one another to help each other through this. That's the key."

"It's not as easy as you think. I don't think love is the problem. It never was," Sylvia told her. "I've always loved Garry, and I always will."

"No one said it was easy. Hell, I don't know any woman who can be dealing with this situation and handling it the way that you are. You are to be commended. Talk to me."

Sylvia looked at her friend and said, "I don't think Garry feels like he can talk to me."

"What? What do you mean?"

"He met Miranda when his father died. Garry never mentioned his father being alive and never mentioned him dying. He says he didn't want to burden me with all of that. But I'm his wife. I'm supposed to be the one that he shares his burdens with, and he didn't."

"Okay, and he's apologized for that," Lynne reminded her.

"It's not just that. It's something else. In the letter, Miranda talked about how they became friends and were able to share with one another. Garry never complains about anything—not his job, not his health, his friends, nothing. He always says everything is fine. I know we have lived a good life, but it could not have been that good. He doesn't talk to me, and I never realized that until this happened. How can I be married to a man who loves me but can't trust me with his innermost feelings?"

"Maybe he's protecting you, Sylvia."

"I don't want to be protected. I'm not some fragile china doll that will break under the pressure of him telling me he's having a bad day at work," Sylvia told her. "And I don't know what else he's keeping from me. Take Jordan, for example."

"She's no longer a secret."

"But it's still something he's not telling me. He keeps threatening her about something, and it's just weird. I can't put my finger on it."

"I think you should talk to him and ask him what's going on. There's no way he can expect you to move forward if he doesn't tell you everything. You need to tell him that you can handle it and it's the only way you are going to be able to rebuild the trust. Now, buy those shoes so you can wear them when you walk down the aisle."

Sylvia looked at the shoes. She didn't know if she would be wearing them down the aisle, but she decided to buy them just in case, along with two other pairs that she liked.

She was surprised that Garry wasn't home by the time she made it to the house later that evening. She checked in Jordan's room and saw that she was gone too.

"Garry and Jordan aren't back yet, Aunt Connie?"

"Nope. I was gonna order some Chinese food, but I didn't know if y'all had eaten."

"That sounds good. Let me call and see if they've eaten."

She went to call Garry, but before she could dial his number, he walked through the door.

"Hey, sweetie, I was just about to call you. Did you and Jordan eat yet? We are about to order Chinese."

"I haven't eaten, but I don't know about Jordan. You have to ask her."

Sylvia looked beyond her husband to see if Jordan was still outside. "Where is she?"

"What do you mean, where is she? Isn't she here?"

They both turned and looked at Aunt Connie.

"She ran out of here a couple of hours ago saying she was going with her dad," Aunt Connie answered.

Sylvia looked at her watch. It was almost six o'clock. Garry pulled out his phone and dialed a number that Sylvia knew had to be Jordan's. She wasn't surprised when he said she didn't answer.

"This girl is gonna be the death of me," Garry growled.

"Garry, wait. I know how to find her," Sylvia said. "When Jordan pulled her little disappearing act the other week, I figured it wouldn't be the last time we would deal with that situation, so I had Kenny put a GPS tracking app on both their phones without them knowing."

"You what? You put a LoJack on her phone?" Garry stared at her.

"Yes, I did." Sylvia nodded.

"Well, that was kinda smart," Aunt Connie said.

"Why didn't you say anything to me about it? Don't you think that's something you should have told me about?" Garry frowned and folded his arms.

"Excuse me? What did you just say? I know like hell you didn't just say that was something I should have *told* you," Sylvia yelled.

Aunt Connie interrupted them. "Wait a minute, you two. First things first. We need to find Jordan."

"Exactly," Sylvia said.

"So, how do we find out where she is?" Garry asked her. "How does this app work?"

"I don't know. I have to call Kenny," Sylvia admitted, taking the phone from Garry and dialing Kenny's number. She quickly told him what was going on, and he told her it was no problem and he was on his way.

"You went through all this trouble and don't know how to even work the damn app? We have to wait on Kenny to get here?" Garry began pacing.

Sylvia knew to walk away before she said something she would regret. She had intended to have Kenny show how her to use the app when he installed it, but she had been so focused on trying to sneak Jordan's phone back into her room without her noticing it was gone that she forgot to ask. It had been hard enough sneaking it out while she was in the shower one evening.

"He knows you meant well. He's just upset. You know that," Aunt Connie came behind her and said.

"It doesn't matter anymore."

"What do you mean?"

"It means just that," Sylvia told her and went upstairs to wait on Kenny.

She entered her office and sat at her desk. She reached into her drawer and took out the letter from Miranda. For what seemed like the hundredth time, she read it. The words were still the same, but the sentiments seemed different somehow. The more she read it, the angrier she became.

"Syl, Kenny is here!" Garry yelled from downstairs.

She folded the letter up and went downstairs.

"Hey, Syl." Kenny took his iPad out of his bag and turned it on.

"Do you know where she is?" Sylvia asked.

"Yeah, I located her," he told her.

"Where is she?" Garry asked.

Kenny held the screen so they all could see it. Sylvia stared at what looked like a map of the entire state with a flashing dot in the center.

"Where is that?" Garry looked closer.

"She's in Madison," Kenny told them.

How they managed to make it to Madison, which was over four hours away, within three hours was beyond Sylvia. It most likely had to do with Garry's complete disregard for the posted speed limits on the highway. She and Kenny had jumped into the car with him, leaving Aunt Connie at the house, promising not to alert Jordan that they were on their way. Once they made it to the city, Kenny's iPad directed them to the coliseum.

"There must be a concert going on," Sylvia said, looking at the rows and rows of cars filling the parking lot and the crowds of people.

"I think it's a game," Kenny said.

"It's a basketball game," Garry commented. "The state championship game is here tonight. Jordan's old school is playing."

Sylvia looked over at Garry. "How do you know?"

"Because she asked me if she could come to the game."

"When?"

"Earlier this week."

Sylvia couldn't believe her husband. "Why didn't you even mention it?"

"Because I told her no. There was no way I was gonna let her come four hours away for a basketball game."

"And yet, here we are," Sylvia mumbled. "This is something we could have done as a family. I didn't even know anything about this, as usual."

"No, we couldn't have. Peyton already had plans."

"She could have changed them," Sylvia yelled.

"Hey, how about you guys get out at the door and I will go park?" Kenny suggested.

Garry pulled to the front, and they both got out. They went over to the ticket booth, and the lady informed them that the game was sold out.

"Listen, my daughter is in this building somewhere. I gotta get in," Garry demanded.

"I'm sorry, sir. I don't know what to tell you," the lady said.

Just as Garry was about to snap, Sylvia pulled him away.

Janelle

The score was tied, and only six seconds remained in the game. The gym was going crazy, and it seemed like they were going to go into overtime. Janelle had become so caught up in the excitement of watching Tank play that it was almost enough to distract her from the fact of who his father was. Tank was graceful and powerful on the floor, and each time he shot the ball, it was with precision. For Janelle, it was like watching a gazelle. Over and over, she watched him run up and down the court, face full of determination. Although she tried not to recognize it, she saw a lot of Titus in him. The crowd cheered louder as the clock continued to count down. Tank went up for an alley-oop, but a player from the opposing team fouled him hard, and he went crashing to the floor.

"Nooooooo!" Janelle screamed along with the rest of the spectators.

The crowd booed and hissed at the player who had fouled him. The referee blew his whistle and motioned for a technical foul, and all eyes were on Tank as he remained still. His coach and fellow players ran to his side, and the gym got quiet.

"God, please let him be all right," Peyton whispered. "Get up, Tank."

As if God and Tank heard her prayer, he stirred. One of the players reached down and helped him up, and the crowd went wild. Janelle breathed a sigh of relief and clapped.

The coach whispered something into his ear. Everyone cleared the floor, and Tank took his place at the free throw line to take the two shots he was afforded. Peyton grabbed Janelle's arm, and they held onto one another and watched in anticipation. He slowly bounced the ball, stared intensely, and shot it toward the basket. It hit the rim and went around and around, then came back out without going through the net.

"Nooooooooo!" Peyton squeezed her arm.

"Ouch, girl!" Janelle flinched.

Half the crowd groaned, while the other half cheered. The referee passed the ball back to Tank, who bounced it again. This time, he inhaled deeply, closed his eyes, and slowly released the ball. It didn't even hit the rim; instead, it swished through the net with ease. The crowd went wild, and Janelle saw the score read 89–90 in favor of Tank's team. All over the gym, people screamed as the clock continued counting down. As the buzzer sounded, people bum-rushed the floor. Peyton hugged Janelle, and they jumped up and down.

"They won! They won!" Peyton screamed. "He did it!"

Janelle looked down to see Tank being carried on the shoulders of his teammates. She couldn't help but smile. Not only was she glad that she had brought her niece to the game, but she had gotten to witness this moment as well.

"Tank! Tank!" an older woman yelled and made her way through the crowd.

"Mom!" Tank smiled as he was lowered to the floor. He ran over and hugged the woman.

It was then that Janelle noticed the man behind her reaching for the boy. She watched as Titus embraced his son and they both cried. She fought the tears she felt forming.

She sighed and said to Peyton, "Come on. Let's go."

"Should I go say something to him?" Peyton asked.

"I doubt if we can get down there," Janelle said, trying not to panic. She knew if Peyton went to see Tank, there was a strong chance they would run into Titus and his wife. That was something she didn't want to risk. "He knows you were here. I'm sure he will call you."

"Yeah, he will." Peyton nodded, and they headed down the bleachers.

They had almost made it to the bottom when suddenly, they heard someone yelling for Peyton. They stopped and looked as the crowd in front of them parted and Tank came running toward them. He lifted her niece off the ground into his arms and kissed her.

"Awwwww!" the crowd cheered.

"Peyton! Peyton!" The voice came over the crowd.

Janelle looked up, and her eyes met Titus's. For a second, she thought maybe he had been the one calling Peyton's name, but then she realized it was a woman's voice. Janelle turned and saw her sister rushing toward them. At that same moment, she heard another name being called and looked across the floor.

"Jordan! Get over here now!" It was Garry.

Janelle scanned the crowd to see where he was headed, and she saw that Jordan was standing near the middle of the floor.

"Dad?" Jordan looked shocked to see her father. She jumped behind the man standing beside her.

Janelle saw the look of anger on Garry's face as he charged toward them. She looked from Jordan to the man, who was bracing himself to face Garry.

It was then that her eyes met with his. She frowned and said, "Sherrod?"

Before Sherrod could respond, Garry grabbed him by the collar, and the two me began fighting. Janelle tried to run over, screaming Garry's name and demanding that he stop. She grabbed at Garry, and he pushed her out of the way. Janelle fell to the floor.

That's when she heard Titus calling her name and pushing his way through the crowd with his son right behind him. She looked up to see him swinging at Garry, and she screamed. An all-out brawl ensued.

"Are you okay?" Janelle looked up and saw Kenny standing in front of her car, where she had been sitting on the hood.

"Is that a rhetorical question?" she asked him.

He walked over and sat beside her. "Not really. I mean, are you physically hurt in any way? I know your mind gotta be effed up."

"I am physically fine." Janelle nodded. Although she had hit the ground, her body wasn't hurt at all. But Kenny was right; her mind was all over the place, and she had been sitting in the parking lot trying to think. "What the hell just happened?" she asked. "Security wouldn't let me talk to anyone. They told me I had to leave. Where is Garry, Sylvia, and the girls? I don't know where Titus is. I don't know anything."

"The fam is still inside. I don't know where Titus went. I do know that no one is pressing charges. Although Garry was going on and on about that dude that was with Jordan," Kenny told her.

"Sherrod."

"You know him? Did you know he knew Jordan?"

"Yeah, I know him, but I didn't know he knew Jordan. I mean, how would he?"

"Maybe you can ask him, because it looks like he's headed over here." Kenny nodded in the direction, and Janelle saw Sherrod coming toward them.

She stood up and folded her arms.

"What's up?" he said. His hands were stuffed inside the sweatshirt, and he looked as confused as she felt.

"Sherrod, what the hell is going on? How do you know Garry and Jordan? Wait, before you answer that, are you okay?" Janelle asked, noticing the slight swelling and redness on his face.

"I'm good," he told her.

"Good. Now, can you tell me what the hell is going on?"

Sherrod looked over to Kenny, who was still sitting on Janelle's car, listening. "Man, this is crazy. Can we go somewhere and talk in private?"

"No, talk now. That's Kenny. He's family," Janelle told him.

"What's up?" Kenny nodded.

"I've known Jordan since the day she was born. She's like a daughter to me, and the reason I moved was to be near her."

"What?" Janelle asked, now even more confused.

"Randy—Miranda, her mother, was my best friend. I helped raise her. Well, until Randy died," Sherrod told her with tears in his eyes.

"Oh, damn," Kenny said.

"Garry said Jordan didn't have anyone else in her life." Janelle shook her head.

"That's because Garry didn't want me to be in Jordan's life. He never has. I didn't like the fact that Randy had a baby by a married man, and I let it be known. We've bumped heads several times. Hell, not only did he try to tell Randy he didn't like her being my friend, but he tried to forbid me from spending time with Jordan, until Randy let him know he was out of his mind. It was a constant battle, and then when Randy died, I guess he figured he had finally won. But I transferred stores to be near her. I love that girl like no one else in the world."

"Why didn't you say anything before?" Janelle asked him.

"I was going to, but it never seemed like the right time. As a matter of fact, I was going to ask you if the law firm you work for handles complicated custody matters when we went out again, but I didn't get the chance to even ask you out. I want to fight for custody. She's miserable living in that house."

Janelle leaned back on her car and tried to process everything Sherrod had told her. As complicated as it sounded, it made sense.

"I still can't believe you brought her all the way here without anyone's permission." Janelle shook her head, "That was wrong, and you know it."

"If I hadn't brought her, she was gonna run away and come anyway. I figured it would be safer if I drove her here, and we would deal with the consequences when she got back. I know that sounds immature, but it is what it is. No one expected any of this to happen."

"No one ever does," Janelle told him.

Sherrod took a step toward her. "Janelle, I'm sorry."

Janelle held her hand up to stop him from coming any closer. "Me too, but I think you need to leave."

"Can I call you?" he asked.

"Let me deal with this, and I will talk to you soon, Sherrod," she told him, and he walked away.

After what seemed like hours, she finally said to Kenny, "Can you believe this?"

"Well, I do believe him," Kenny said.

"Why?"

Kenny turned and said, "Because Randy said so in her letter."

"What letter?"

"The letter she wrote to your sister before she died."

Sylvia

"Are you going to church?" Garry asked, sitting on the sofa where he had slept the night before. He'd had enough sense not to even try to get in the bed with her.

Sylvia looked at the clock and saw that it was almost nine in the morning. She hadn't even been to sleep, and she knew he hadn't either. If he had, she would have heard him snoring. Instead, she listened as he tossed and turned for most of the night.

They hadn't gotten home until well after three. The drive had been completely silent, with the exception of the occasional sniff from either Jordan or Peyton, both of whom had been crying. Sylvia didn't have the energy or the desire to try to comfort either one of them.

"No," she answered and pulled the covers tighter around her.

"Do you want to talk now?" he asked.

"No."

Sylvia had decided that there was no point in talking. Last night proved that Garry only shared what he felt she needed to know. And, as much as she thought she knew, Sylvia really didn't know anything. She didn't know who this strange man was her husband had attacked at the basketball game. She didn't know the boy who had so passionately kissed Peyton in front of the entire world. She didn't know her sister had driven Peyton to the game. Her life was so full of unknowns and secrets that she could barely see straight.

"We are going to have to talk, Sylvia," Garry told her. "And we need to do it before we deal with Jordan and Peyton. We need to be on the same page."

"What page is that, Garry? The page where you've already dictated and decided what's going to happen, leaving out the parts of the story that you don't want anyone else to read?" Sylvia snapped, sitting up in the bed.

"What are you talking about?" Garry questioned.

"Why didn't you tell me about Sherrod? Isn't that his name?" Sylvia recalled hearing the man giving his name to the officers when they were taken to the back office of the arena.

"I didn't even know he was here. And I told Jordan that she wasn't supposed to have any contact with him," Garry told her.

"It doesn't matter where he was. You should've told me about him. And you should've explained why you didn't want Jordan to be in contact with him."

"I didn't think it was something to bother you with, Sylvia. I wanted you to focus on our marriage and putting it back together."

"See, that's the problem. You want to leave out the bits and pieces that are key to the whole broken puzzle. But you want to put it back together? That's not how it works. Why is it that you can't talk to me?" She began crying.

Garry rushed and sat beside her, reaching for her hand, which she snatched away.

"I'm trying to talk you. You are the one who said you didn't want to."

Sylvia shook her head and told him, "I don't know who you are anymore. I thought I did, but I don't."

"What do you mean?"

"Why did Sherrod and Miranda's friendship bother you so much, Garry? Tell me."

"Because I didn't like him, and I didn't want him around my daughter. He made me uncomfortable."

"Why? It was her best friend. He loved your daughter as much as you did. He was there for Randy when you couldn't be. So, what was the problem? Were you in love with Randy?"

"What? No! Have you lost your mind?"

"Was he in love with Randy?"

"I don't know. I don't care." Garry suddenly stood up.

Sylvia shook her head. "You have an affair a decade and a half ago with Miranda, who ends up pregnant and gives birth to your kid. You never mention anything about any of this, and the only reason I find out is because of a horrible accident. That's one thing, and now you're getting into fist fights in public. Miranda was right; you're dealing with some deep-rooted issues that you need to figure out." Sylvia's words were sharp and forceful. She was beyond frustrated and so fed up with him that she didn't realize what she'd said until Garry stepped back and gave her a questioning gaze.

"What do you mean, Miranda was right?" His voice was barely above a whisper.

Sylvia blinked for a few moments, suddenly aware of the information she'd inadvertently divulged. "You're missing the point, Garry. Your behavior last night—"

"And you're deflecting. Now, answer my question. What did you mean?"

There was no turning back. She hadn't planned on telling Garry like this, but there was no way she could complain about his withholding information and then do the same thing. She wasn't a liar or a hypocrite.

"Miranda. She said you were controlling and had some issues when it comes to dealing with others."

Garry continued to stare at her, but his next words let her know that this wasn't the first time he'd heard this. "She was wrong. I don't have a problem with the dynamics of shit."

"I didn't say that you did." Sylvia frowned, recalling other statements Miranda had made in the letter.

"Who did Miranda supposedly say this to? Don't tell me: that asshole Sherrod. I swear he—"

"He didn't do or say anything. She told me herself," Sylvia finally said.

"Sylvia, what the hell are you talking about?"

"She left me a letter," Sylvia told him. "Before she passed. She wrote it years ago, it seems."

"That's crazy. I don't understand. How did you get it?" Garry shook his head in disbelief.

"She put it in the back of Jordan's baby book, and I found it."

"No, Randy didn't do that. She didn't. This is some shit Sherrod is doing. That's what he does. He tries to make me look bad. He put it there." Garry began pacing back and forth.

"Why do you keep accusing this man? What the hell is wrong with you?" Sylvia was now worried about her husband's behavior. Seeing him physically assault Sherrod had taken her by surprise. She'd never seen him hit anyone. And now, he seemed to be visibly shaken.

"I'm telling you, Syl, whatever is in that letter isn't true. He's crazy and a liar." Garry was breathing so hard that Sylvia could see his chest rising and falling.

She turned and rushed out of the bedroom.

He called behind her. "Syl, where are you going? We're not finished."

She didn't stop until she was in her office. Reaching into the bottom drawer of her file cabinet, she quickly searched under the pile of nuptial magazines and publications until she found her wedding planner and flipped to the back where she kept the letter. When she was trying to think of a place to keep it, it had seemed like a fitting and ironic place.

Sylvia stood up and closed the drawer with her foot with a little more force than she had intended. It closed with a loud bang, and she hoped it didn't wake Peyton or Aunt Connie, whose bedrooms were right down the hall.

When she walked back into the bedroom, Garry was sitting on the side of the bed, looking lost and bewildered.

"Here." She handed him the envelope, now wrinkled from being opened so many times.

"What is this?" Garry just stared at her hand in front of him.

"Take it. It's the letter full of lies," Sylvia said. "The one you said Sherrod wrote."

"I don't want it." Garry shook his head.

"No, take it and read it. Read all the lies in there about you." Sylvia forced the letter into his hands.

After a few seconds, he finally took it from her and pulled out the crumpled letter. She watched his face as he read it.

July 11, 2001
11:11 p.m.

Dear Sylvia,
If you're reading this, it means that somehow, someway, I have finally found the nerve to reach out to you and reveal those things that have been hidden after all this time. I guess I should start by introducing myself. My name is Miranda Meachum, affectionately known to many as Randy. I currently hold a position as the head mixologist at Salute, one of the most prestigious bars in the city, where I've worked for the past several years. I am a master wine sommelier by trade. I take pride in everything I do, including my love of scrapbooking, HGTV, and most of all, my wonderful daughter and love of my life, Jordan, who was fathered by your husband, Garry.

I make no apologies for the birth of my child. Although her conception wasn't one that was planned, it happened nevertheless. Garry and I met under circumstances that were saddened and haunted by the death of two very important people in our lives: his father and my fiancé. We shared one night of forgettable sex, and I say that in the most respectable way possible, because truly, each one of us barely remembers it. What I do remember is being sad, lonely, and wanting to die. I had lost a part of me that I felt I couldn't live without, and my desire to live was gone. I had nothing to live for.

And then, one day as I sat looking at a calendar, trying to plan which day I would take my own life (as if whether I committed suicide on a day I was scheduled to work would make a difference), I realized that I hadn't had a period in some time. I took a pregnancy test, and when it came back positive, I was elated, thinking that somehow God had allowed my fiancé to live by blessing me with our baby. In the midst of planning my baby shower a few months later, it occurred to me that there was a slight chance that Garry may have fathered my child.

I contemplated, and against the advice of my closest friend, I called and told him. He was shocked, but he handled the news well, from what I could tell. I assured him that I would let him know. On the day my daughter was born, I called, and he came to the hospital. He knew, as well as I did, that she was his. He asked that I name her Jordan and promised she would be cared for. He also told me he was happily married.

Over the years, Garry has done what he promised from that first day. He has been a great father, provider, and friend. Jordan has had to celebrate Christmas some years on the twenty-seventh of December, and Valentine's Day sometimes on February twelfth, but she is always celebrated and acknowledged. The times he missed those important dance recitals, cheerleading competitions, and other milestones have been few and far between.

Despite the circumstances, Garry is to be commended. He has made co-parenting a breeze. In all that he has done right, however, there have been some things that he's done wrong. His controlling nature has at times taken a toll on my friendship with others, especially males. He's dealing with some deep-rooted hurt that has resulted in his inability to understand the dynamics of friendship, and I'm worried about him. He is a troubled man, and it bothers me to see him like this. I know that he loves you very much. Maybe the burden of fathering Jordan is weighing him down. Maybe the secret is taking its toll on him, and maybe, once the truth is finally out, he can find some much-needed peace in his life.

I wish both of you nothing but the best in your lives, your family, and your marriage. His love for you is enduring and one of a kind. Hold on to it. A love like that is rare, but it is powerful enough to overcome mistakes, hurt, and it's not easily destroyed. Even in death, I still feel the love my fiancé and I shared, and I know that we will be together one day.

Blessings,
Miranda "Randy" Meachum

"She was an amazing woman. Under any other circumstances, I probably would have loved to have met her. You're right. She was your friend and a great mother, and I know that because only a real friend who loved their child would've written such lies, as you put it."

"Syl, I'm so sorry."

"I'm sick of hearing that from you. I want you out of here, Garry. I can't do this anymore," she told him with tears in her eyes. "Until you feel like you can be open and honest with me about everything, we don't need to be together."

"I do feel that way," Garry pleaded. "I've told you everything."

"No, you're not. There's something you're not telling me. I don't know what it is, but I know there is. I thought we were going to be able to do this together, but I can't, Garry. It's too much."

Garry rushed over, grabbing her shoulders. "Sylvia, don't do this to me. I need you; I need my family. You can't kick us out. Jordan, she needs stability and structure and we . . . we need you. She just lost one mother."

Sylvia hated that he was playing on her sympathy and using Miranda's death to make her change her mind. "I know this, which is why I tried."

"Sylvia, I can't lose her." Garry was crying and sweating at this point. "Please don't make me lose her. I can't let that bastard have her. I can't."

"Garry, for God's sake, tell me what the hell you're talking about. Lose who?" Sylvia asked him.

"Sherrod. He's going to file for custody of Jordan," Garry told her. "And he says Randy wrote him a letter too."

The ringing of the doorbell stopped Sylvia before she could respond. She looked at Garry and said, "Who in the world could that be?"

Garry pulled a T-shirt out of his drawer, and Sylvia jumped up and slipped on her robe and slippers before they both went downstairs. Sylvia peeked out of the window and took a step back when she saw who was standing on the other side of the door. It was the last person she would have ever expected, especially after what had happened the night before.

"Who is it?" Garry asked her.

Sylvia unlocked the door and opened it. She stared at the woman for a few moments, neither one saying a word, until Sylvia finally broke the awkward silence by saying, "Good morning."

"We need to talk. Can I come inside?"

Sylvia glanced at her husband, who gave her a strange look then shrugged. Moving to the side and motioning for her to come in, Sylvia welcomed Titus's wife inside their home.

To be continued in

Imitation of Wife

coming in August 2019

Please enjoy the preview on the next page!

Sylvia

"Um, come in," Sylvia said, moving to the side so her unexpected guest could walk in. Her eyes met Garry's. He looked just as surprised.

"I'm sorry to just show up like this, but I . . . I tried calling your daughter and she didn't answer and I . . . I . . ." She began crying.

"What's going on?" Aunt Connie rushed into the foyer and over to the crying woman. "What's got you so upset?"

"Uh, Aunt Connie, this is Tricia," Sylvia told her. "She's . . ." Sylvia didn't know how to introduce her. Her day was getting more and more awkward by the minute. It seemed that the turmoil from last night was overflowing, and before she could wrap her mind around one thing, another one popped up. Certainly, Titus's wife was here to talk about her husband and Janelle. She was dressed in a pair of sweats and Timberland boots, which Sylvia hoped wasn't an indication that she planned on fighting

"Tarik, uh, Tank's mom," Tricia said, wiping her eyes. "He and Peyton are friends."

"Garry, go get some Kleenex," Aunt Connie instructed, and Garry didn't hesitate to rush off. Sylvia was sure he was relieved to be able to leave the three of them. "Come on in here and sit down."

Sylvia tried to subtly get her aunt's attention, but she was too busy leading Tricia into the living room. The two of them sat on the sofa, while Sylvia sat in a nearby chair.

"Here you go." Garry eased in the room, holding out a box of Kleenex.

"Thank you," Tricia said, snatching several out and wiping her eyes.

"Okay, now tell us, why are you crying, baby?" Aunt Connie coaxed her.

"Because Tank is missing. After the incident at the game last night, he and his father had words. He rode the bus back to the school with the team, but he didn't come home. We've looked all over for him." She sniffed. "I've talked to all of his friends, but they don't know where he is."

"So, you came here?" Sylvia looked at her like she was crazy. "You think he's here?"

"I . . . I don't know. Like I said, I tried calling and texting Peyton. She didn't answer. And I have been driving everywhere. I'm sorry for showing up like this." Tricia began crying all over again.

Garry, who was standing in the doorway, said, "I can tell you right now he's not here. Peyton is upstairs asleep."

"Why don't you go wake her up and see if she's heard from her li'l boyfriend?" Aunt Connie suggested. "What's his name? Frank?"

"Tank," Garry corrected her, adding, "her *friend*."

"I'll go talk to her," Sylvia volunteered, but at that moment, both Peyton and Jordan came walking down the steps. Sylvia was taken aback, since Jordan's room was downstairs, and she rarely ventured to the second floor of their home. She was wearing a pair of leggings and a nightshirt. Peyton had on a pair of shorts and an unfamiliar T-shirt, which was too big. Sylvia noticed Tank's basketball number emblazoned on the back and wondered when and where she'd gotten it.

"What's going on?" Jordan asked.

"Mrs. King?" Peyton's eyes widened when she saw Tricia sitting on the sofa beside Aunt Connie.

"Peyton, when's the last time you talked to Tank?" Garry asked her.

"Um, I talked to him last night after the game. He was pretty upset about what happened," Peyton said. "I kinda don't blame him."

Tricia stood up. "What did he say? What time did you talk to him?"

"I . . . I'm not sure. He said he was gonna call me later today," Peyton said. "What's wrong?"

"Baby, Tank didn't come home last night. His parents are worried," Sylvia explained.

"He's probably with somebody from the team partying. We did win the state championship last night, remember?" Jordan sneered and folded her arms. "Not that they got the chance to celebrate and enjoy the moment like they should have. Someone stopped that from happening."

"Not now, Jordan," Garry warned.

"I'm just saying," Jordan said. "You ruined his moment."

"Peyton, sweetie, maybe you can run upstairs and get your phone and see if he's tried to call, or maybe see if you can reach him," Sylvia suggested.

Peyton looked over at Jordan for a moment, then back to her mother and said, "Okay. I'll be right back."

"I'm sure he's fine," Aunt Connie said. "Both Peyton and Jordan here snuck off yesterday and we found them. And Peyton went off for a couple of hours the other week and we couldn't find her, and she showed up at home."

Sylvia gave Aunt Connie the same warning Garry had given Jordan moments before. "Not now, Aunt Connie."

"He probably just needs to cool off, that's all." Jordan shrugged. "I do that all the time. I take a time out."

"Has he ever gone missing before?" Sylvia asked.

"No, never." Tricia shook her head. "I've never seen him so angry and disappointed. And she's right; last night should've been the biggest moment of Tank's life. He's worked and trained so hard."

"Yeah, and after that horrible loss last year when the refs cheated, he deserved this," Jordan said.

"Wait, you know Tank too?" Garry asked.

"Yeah, by association," Jordan answered. "He's a friend of a friend."

"Did you know he and Peyton were—" Sylvia paused and glanced at Garry before completing her sentence. "Friends?"

"No, not until everything popped off last night after the game. Like I told you, she and I aren't cool like that. We don't talk," Jordan said.

"But you stayed in her room last night, didn't you?" Sylvia asked.

"You did?" Garry sounded surprised.

"No, I didn't." Jordan turned her nose up in disgust. "I stayed in Aunt Connie's room."

Sylvia looked over at Aunt Connie to confirm.

"She did come and sleep with me last night. She was upset and needed to talk about what happened." Aunt Connie shook her head at Garry.

"He didn't answer." Peyton came back down with her cell phone in hand. "I sent him a text, but it wasn't delivered. His phone must be dead."

"Oh my God. I don't know where he could be." Tricia began crying again, and Aunt Connie stood and rubbed her back.

"I'll be right back," Sylvia said and exited the room. She was halfway up the stairs when she heard Garry behind her.

"Syl, where are you going?" he hissed. "You can't leave a hysterical woman in our living room."

"I said I'd be right back," she whispered as she kept walking. "I have a phone call to make."

"Who the hell are you calling?" He followed her into their bedroom.

Sylvia picked up her cell phone and pressed her sister's name.

"What?" Janelle answered after the third ring.

"Nelle, wake up. We have a situation," Sylvia told her.

"You're calling Janelle? That's the last person you need to be calling right now considering who's downstairs," Garry said.

"Shut up, Garry. You're the last person who needs to be talking to me right now considering everything," she snapped at him.

He sulked but didn't say anything else.

"What the hell is going on? What time is it?" Janelle groaned.

"Nelle, I need you to call Titus right now," Sylvia told her. "Call him on three-way. I need to talk to him."

"I'm not calling him. Why do you want him?" Janelle asked.

"Because his wife is downstairs crying in my living room," Sylvia said, trying not to yell.

"Shit. What?" Janelle squealed. "What the hell for? Why is she there? Is she looking for me?"

"No, she's not looking for you. She's looking for her son. Now, call him."

"What? Tank is at your house?"

"Janelle." It was taking everything for Sylvia not to snap, and she was two seconds from losing it. "I don't have time to play no damn twenty-one questions. Get Titus's ass on the phone, *now*."

"Fine. Hold on," Janelle said, and then the phone went quiet.

"Go downstairs and check and see what's going on," Sylvia told Garry.

"I'm sure Tricia's still crying, Jordan is still complaining, Peyton is still moping, and Aunt Connie has it all under control," he said. "They don't need me down there."

Although she knew her husband was probably right, she told him, "Well, I don't need you up here either."

"Hello?" Titus's voice came on the line. "Syl, what's going on? Tricia's at your house?"

"Yes, she is. She's out frantically looking for your son," Sylvia told him.

"Oh my God. I told her to relax and don't panic." Titus sighed.

"Wait, do you know where he is?" Sylvia asked, wondering why he seemed so calm while Tricia was about to damn near have a heart attack in her living room.

"No, not really," Titus said.

"What the hell does that mean? No, not really? Have you talked to him?" Sylvia was now talking through clenched teeth.

"No, I haven't talked to him, but I don't think he's run away anywhere. His clothes are still in his room, and he knows he has a news interview at three o'clock this afternoon. Besides, the entire school will be celebrating the team at school tomorrow, and he ain't missing that. He's just mad at me right now. And I get that," Titus told her.

"I can't believe you aren't worried the least bit," Janelle spoke up. She'd been so quiet that Sylvia forgot she was on the phone.

"He's a teenage boy who was publicly embarrassed by his father. Home was the last place he wanted to be," Titus told her.

"You need to check on your wife," Sylvia said, thinking about how upset Tricia was and remembering how upset she had felt when Peyton went missing. "You're acting like it's no big deal when really, you don't know."

"I'll call her and tell her to come home," Titus said; then he said, "Has she said anything else?"

"Like what?" Sylvia asked.

"Like, about anyone else?" His voice was barely audible.

"No, Titus, she hasn't said anything about my sister, your mistress, if that's what you're referring to. And frankly, I don't blame her." Sylvia hung up the phone. The nerve of him to even ask her that question. He was just as selfish as her husband.

She brushed past Garry and said, "We still have unfinished business from this morning. This doesn't change anything."